FUEL

DirtSlap Series
By
Ashlynn Pearce

FUEL

FUEL Copyright © 2015 Ashlynn Pearce
Smashwords Edition
ALL RIGHTS RESERVED
Published by: Whimsy Notions Press, LLC
Cover artist: PickymeArtist.com[1]
Editor: Labelle's Writing on the Wall
Formatting: BB eBooks

With the exception of quotes used in reviews, this book may not be reproduced or used in whole or in part by any means existing without written permission from the publisher, Whimsy Notions Press, LLC.

This book is a work of fiction and any resemblance to persons, living or dead, or places, events or locales is purely coincidental. The characters are productions of the author's imagination and used fictitiously.

Use of artists and song titles are done so for storytelling purposes and should in no way be seen as advertisement. Trademark names are used in an editorial fashion with no intention of infringement of the respective owner's trademark.

Table of Contents

Dedication

To my man...*for always being there. You're in every hero I write.*
I love you.
To my girls...
Linda ~ for always being there. Never letting me give up and
keeping me sane through some of the darkest days of my life.
Nichol ~ for being my first ever fan and becoming a best friend.
You know I couldn't have done this without you!
Silver ~ for being the best cheerleader a girl could ask for.
Jennifer ~ For being an inspiration and always telling me I can
do it. Can I be you when I grow up?
To every person who reads my stories.
Thank you.
It's been a long road getting back and I cherish that you've
taken the time to buy and read my books.
Love and happy reading/writing!

Chapter 1

Free.

She was finally free.

The air brakes hissed as the bus came to a stop at the depot. Cassie Dalton stepped off for the first time since she'd boarded nine hours ago. She tightened her long ponytail and walked down the sidewalk to peer around the bus. Her hometown was barely big enough for a high school, much less the multiple story buildings that stretched into Nashville's blue sky.

She took a deep breath and closed her eyes. The warmth from the Tennessee sun relaxed her and she shook off all she'd left behind. Her life started now.

She rubbed the worn, brown leather cuff on her left wrist. *This is for you, Cam.*

She'd done it. She wouldn't spend another birthday in that slow as molasses po-dunk town. She'd barely resisted flipping off Oklahoma when she crossed the state line. Now, she was headed to New York, with a one-way ticket.

She was more than ready to start her new life.

Everything she owned fit in a backpack and duffle bag. She didn't need much. With those bags in hand and a couple of hours before the next bus would show, she walked to a nearby convenience store, grabbed a sandwich, a bottle of water, and sat beneath a tree.

The late spring breeze ruffled her hair and fluffy clouds dotted the sky. She'd expected Nashville to be cold concrete.

Instead, the city burst through the trees and blended seamlessly into the countryside. Unlike Memphis, with its raw edgy feel, Nashville was a gem in a midst of green.

She glanced at the time on her phone and frowned. She got up, stepped into the mostly empty bus station and moved to the office window.

"Isn't the next bus to New York supposed to be here already?" she asked the tiny man behind the counter.

He blinked at her, his eyes huge behind the lenses of his glasses. "Seems there's been a problem. Your next bus won't be here until tomorrow afternoon at two."

"Why?"

"Bus broke down."

She sighed. "Guess I'm stuck here for the night."

She took a glimpse of the skyline. Not a bad place to spend her twenty-first birthday. It was light years from Woodbridge Grove, Oklahoma. And that was good enough for her.

After she checked into a cheap motel, she roamed down Honky Tonk Row ready to celebrate her freedom, and her birthday. She'd never had much to be happy about, but now she couldn't stop the smile that tugged at her lips. Even though it was Wednesday, the place was hopping...at least to her it was. She'd never seen so many people, in one place, in all her life.

Music poured out of each bar, club, and restaurant she passed. She paused to take it all in. A couple of bars over a band played a cover of Jason Aldean's *Crazy Town* and it had her tapping her worn boots. The tune seemed more than appropriate, so she followed the sound.

The bouncer at the door stopped her, asked for ID, then grinned when he looked at it.

"Twenty-one today, huh?" he said more than asked.

"Yep. Is that a probl—"

"Hey, Cliff," the bouncer yelled into the bar, "you got a virgin here."

Cassie froze at his choice of words and was hauled inside by one of the laughing waitresses. "Ah, you look as fresh as they come, sweetie."

The woman shoved her onto a barstool and the bartender slapped the wood right in front of her so hard it made her jump. "Ooowee! So you're the virgin, huh?"

She blinked as heat crawled up her cheeks. She hoped they were talking about her birthday and not something else. But she couldn't tell because the music was deafening, and she had gathered a crowd. A crowd that hooped and hollered around her, making her ears ring.

"No one with you, darling?" asked Cliff.

She shook her head.

He lowered dark brows and gave her a knowing smirk.

"Well, you won't be alone for long." He poured her a shot. "Bottoms up. Virgin, you'll be no more."

With the partygoers chanting bottoms up, she warily picked up the glass and downed it. She choked on the burn that sizzled all the way to her toes. But as people roared in approval and clapped her on the back, she tossed her head on a laugh. For the first time in her life, she didn't worry about who might judge her. She didn't have to keep a look out over her shoulder for the next snide remark or, even worse, for her dad's next slap. She couldn't live like that anymore.

And vowed she never would.

With a group of strangers, she could be herself.

"Cliff, give me another one." Her voice rang clear with confidence and her heart beat fast with the knowledge she could make her own rules.

He happily set her up.

Cassie was having the time of her life. Not once did she have to pay for a drink. And if she wanted to dance, countless guys stood in line to fill the role. They'd told her their names, but she hadn't paid enough attention to remember them. Not until one guy, Mason, who kept slipping his hands where she didn't want them.

The bar became downright suffocating, and she needed some air, so she stepped outside. She made her way toward the Cumberland River to breathe and clear her head but hadn't gotten very far when an arm wrapped around her waist. She turned in time for lips to land on hers.

She was lit, but her instincts were still intact from years of having to fight for herself. She sunk her teeth into his lip. The guy yelped, loosened his grip and she brought her elbow hard into his face.

Slippery hands Mason, she sneered and was about to kick him in the nuts when someone stepped between them.

"Hey, dude, back off. I don't think she wants your attention."

Cassie's brows furrowed as her fuzzy brain latched onto that voice. She stared at the broad back encased in black leather attempting to decipher how she knew him.

"How do you know? Maybe she's playing hard to get," Mason mumbled.

The guy chuckled. "Sure. Like she didn't just bloody your lip. And I think she was about to kick you in nuts. Take a walk, man. You don't want any part of this."

Cassie rubbed her eyes and swayed on her feet. That voice . . . She knew that voice but couldn't place it.

"Darlin', you all right?" The guy had turned toward her and touched her elbow.

She opened her eyes and the blood drained from her face. No. It couldn't be him.

"Hey, you okay?" He cocked his head. "Wait. Do I know you?"

Those familiar blue-gray eyes narrowed as he stared at her. She tried to answer. But the only thing she accomplished was opening her mouth and gaping like an idiot. Happiness, sheer joy, sadness then rage hit her all at once. Every emotion she had kept locked away bubbled to the surface. How the hell had she run into him of all people? It made her head spin worse than all the alcohol she had consumed.

"Thrand," she yelled and balled her fists, ready to punch his shocked face.

"Buzzkill?"

She hadn't heard that nickname in years and her heart constricted. His face blurred through her watery gaze. It was too much. Her stomach rolled and lurched.

Then she threw up on his boots.

Thrand Medlam peeked into the dim bathroom to check on Cassie. She was sitting up, her back against the tub, her elbows resting on her knees, with her head in her hands. Long honey-blonde hair covered her face.

"You all right?" he asked.

"Oh my god. I thought I was awake."

"What?" He put a glass of water and two aspirin on the sink and squatted in front of her. He touched her head. "Cas."

She screeched and jumped so hard she banged her elbow on the tub. "Shit."

He got a glimpse of green eyes through the fall of her hair as she rubbed her arm.

"You're...real. Fuck." She dropped her head back to her knees.

"As real as the vomit I cleaned off my boots." Thrand chuckled.

She groaned. "I really did that?"

"Yup. You also puked in my toilet all night. But it's okay. I think that's how most people spend the morning after turning twenty-one." When she didn't answer or look at him he asked, "Would you like some breakfast?"

"You're joking, right? Unless you want a repeat performance...no."

"Got it." He grabbed the water and aspirin. "Take these and drink. I promise they'll help."

She pushed her hair out of her face and licked her lips.

"I highly doubt it," she muttered but took them. When her hand brushed against his, he stared into her face—the same yet different.

He couldn't believe Cassie Dalton, his best friend's little sister, was in his home. Seven years had passed since he'd last seen her. She'd been fourteen, him nineteen. He never thought he'd see her again.

"Take a shower. I'll get you one of my shirts and some coffee. That should help perk you up." His voice was hoarse. The memories of everything he had left rushed back in force.

"My shirt is fine. Thanks."

"Darlin', I believe it fared worse than my boots."

She looked down. "Ewww...yeah, okay. At least I know what that smell is now. Yes, shower. Clean shirt."

He grabbed her hand and helped her up, putting his other hand on her waist when she swayed into him.

"I'll never drink that much again." She gripped his arm and peered at him.

Her gaze struck him hard. Innocence clung to her face even with a hangover. How had she held onto that when he knew what, or more to the point, who she'd lived with? And he'd left her there to deal with it on her own. Had she gotten the help he'd tried to get for her?

She continued to stare, and he tried to read her thoughts. He knew last night she was ready to hit him. Did she still feel that way? And the biggest question of all, how the hell had she found him?

He stepped back. "I'll get that shirt."

He took the stairs two at a time, headed to his bedroom, pulled the first shirt he found out of his closet, then rushed back down. He dropped the garment on the sink in the bathroom. Cas was already in the shower, her clothes piled on the floor.

Yeah, he was *not* going to think of her naked in his shower because right now, she was anything *but* a buzzkill.

He was making coffee when he heard the barstool slide. He turned and almost dropped his cup. Her hair hung in long, wet strands and she'd tucked his loose shirt into the front into her frayed denim shorts. It brought attention to those mile-long legs and bare feet.

She'd certainly grown up. No longer the lanky, shy girl he'd left, she was a woman who looked him right in the eye. They'd been close back then and seeing her like this blindsided him.

Hot didn't even begin to describe what she was doing to his blood. His friends would call her a long, tall cool one. But she was more like a strong shot of whiskey leaving that same sort of burn.

He placed the cup in front of her as she slid onto the stool.

"Better?" he asked and forced himself to focus on who she was—a girl who had once been a lot like a sister to him.

"Much. Thanks." She took a sip. "Caffeine, the cure for anything."

Her lips curled up slightly and he leaned against the counter.

"So how did you find me?" He'd told no one where he was going when he left Oklahoma and he hadn't talked to any of them since.

"Really? You think I came here looking for you?" She took another drink then straightened her spine, her eyes chips of green ice. "You left. Without a word. Why the hell would I come looking for you?"

"I think it's a little coincidental that you ended up here."

She shoved at her wet hair and choked on a sarcastic laugh. "You're telling me. Trust me, I had no idea you were here. I'm on my way to New York. Transfer bus is supposed to be here at two."

"You're headed to New York? Why?" He had been to New York and no matter how different or tough she seemed, that place would eat her up and spit her out.

"Yeah. No worries. I'll be on a bus headed that way in a few hours. And why not? Anywhere is better than where I was. You should know that. You took off as soon as you could." Venom laced her voice and matched the fire in her eyes.

Oh yeah, she still wanted to punch him.

"Cas, that's no place for you and," he scrubbed his face and sighed. "I tried—"

She held up her hand. "Save it. I really don't care. Just take me to my motel and I won't be a problem for you anymore."

Cassie didn't say much as they got in his truck and headed to her motel. The fourteen-year-old girl she used to be was thrilled beyond belief to see him. The woman she'd become was ticked off.

Unfortunately, that didn't stop her from stealing glances at him. At his house, he'd been wearing nothing but a pair of low-slung jeans and she wasn't immune. He'd filled out quite nicely. She'd thought he was cute before...but now? He was what women posted as wallpaper on their desktops so they could drool on a regular basis.

He'd really thought she was looking for him? How dare he?

He'd left her there to deal with her drunk father. Alone. The last person she ever thought to see again was Thrand Medlam. No way in hell was she about to admit that her first instinct was to hug him and not let him go.

"What do you do here?" She had to say something so she wouldn't fixate on the tattoos that emphasized his arm and made him sexier than he was already.

"Drums. I play in studios and fill in for bands around town now and then."

"You don't have your own band?"

"No. I like what I'm doing. I also write songs. Bartend when it's slow."

He wore a black cap on backwards and dark sunglasses, so she couldn't read his eyes, but his lips twitched. She wasn't sure if he wanted to smile or frown. He also sported a beard clipped close to his face. So short it was just scruff. Her hand itched to test the feel.

She nervously twisted her hair and looked out the window as she pointed to her motel. "Room 54."

"This is where you're staying?" He didn't bother hiding the disdain in his voice and it pissed her off.

She glared at him. "You have a problem with it?"

"Hell yeah, I have a problem." He shoved up his glasses and glared back. "Could you have picked a more unsafe place?"

She lifted her chin in defiance. "It was the best I could do."

She got out and slammed the truck door. She damn sure couldn't wait to be on that bus to New York, because she didn't get out of that hell-hole just to have someone tell her she was doing everything wrong.

She searched through her purse for the key.

"Don't think you need the key." He stepped up and pushed at the door that was already slightly ajar.

The breath left her body as she rushed into her trashed room. Her clothes were strewn all over the place. "No..."

She shoved past Thrand and lifted the mattress where she had hidden her money. Gone. All two thousand she had scraped and saved to get out of Oklahoma was gone.

"No. No. This *cannot* be happening." Her heart thundered in her chest. What the hell would she do now?

"Don't tell me you hid your money between the mattresses? That's the first place they look."

She grit her teeth, willing herself not to cry.

"That was the only place my father wouldn't find my money."

"Ah hell, Cas." Before she could stop him, he'd pulled her up against him in a hug. His arms wrapped tightly around her, his chin resting on her head.

She gave herself a moment to relish it. To let someone else carry her burden. She inhaled his familiar masculine scent. It would be so easy to cling to him. To let him be her rock again. She wiped at a stray tear before she pushed away from him.

"I got some money in my purse. They didn't get it all." Sure, a hundred and fifty bucks. That wouldn't get her very far.

He cocked a brow. "This area's no good. You can stay at my place until you're on your feet. But you're not going to New York."

She clenched her fist, seething at the thought of him ordering her around like she was fourteen again. What she really wanted to do was tell him where he could shove that offer, but she didn't have much choice. She would have to accept help. Just when she thought she could breathe again, she was stuck. With him of all people.

"Fine." She crossed her arms over her chest. "But I won't hang around long. I'll go when and where I want."

He frowned. "Take as long as you need. I have an extra bedroom."

She didn't say anything else but tossed clothes into her bags. She picked up a picture of her brother, Cameron, and Thrand when they were younger and noticed the small frame was broken. She clenched her teeth. Dammit. She would not cry.

Thrand took it from her, shook off the broken glass, and touched Cam's face. Then, without a word, handed it back to her without meeting her gaze.

Getting all her stuff back in her bags didn't take long, but one important thing was missing. She held back the scream that had been slowly building and searched through the tiny room again.

"What else is missing?" His brows furrowed.

She fisted a hand in her hair. "My camera. Looks like they took it, too."

Unable to spend one more minute in the place, she gathered up her meager belongings. She and Thrand got in his truck and were headed to his place before he spoke.

"I know a lot of people here. I can help you get a job."

The windows were down and the warm air whipped her hair wildly around them. She grabbed at the strands and used a ponytail holder to pull it into a messy bun. "I worked at the diner back home for five years."

That earned her a grin that reminded her of the old Thrand. "Ruth & Pops? I loved that place. I still think they had the best root beer floats ever made."

"I remember you and Cam getting run out of there more than once for being too rowdy."

"But they always let us come back. Pops told Ruth we were just being boys."

"Ruth said she let you return because I was always with you guys." She was pretty sure their eyes met, but once again, he had his dark glasses on. She rubbed the leather cuff she wore on her left wrist.

Silence hung heavy between them.

Was he ever going to say anything about Cam's death?

Chapter 2

They had just gotten into his house when the doorbell rang. Thrand opened it and, before he could do anything, Trina threw herself at him and kissed him full on the mouth.

"Where have you been? I wanted to surprise you this morning, but you were already gone."

He forced her back.

Buzzkill cleared her throat. "Hey, I'm Cassie."

"This is Trina," Thrand said and ignored Cassie's accusatory look.

"What's the meaning of this?" Trina asked, hands on her hips. Her eyes narrowed when she spotted Cassie's bags on the couch, then widened when she saw his shirt on Cas. She whipped around to face him and her red face said it all. "This is the final straw, Thrand."

"Final straw? Trina, we were never a couple. You know that." She had to be one of the worse one-night-stand decisions he'd ever made. The only thing she had going for her was big tits.

If it was possible, her face got even redder. "Really? Is that how you see it?"

"Yeah...Maybe you should leave now." With a little smile, Cassie slid up behind him and wrapped her arms around his waist.

Thrand was speechless. All he could concentrate on was the press of Cassie's body against his. Trina cussed him, stomped off and slammed the door. But he was more interested in the girl behind him playing her charade. She looked up at him, her eyes dancing with laughter, her lips curled up just slightly.

"Maybe you should pick your girlfriends better."

He had the urge to taste those lips so close to his and it stunned him. This was Cassie, his best friend's baby sister. The one he'd sworn to protect but had left to fend for herself after Cam had died. There was no way in hell Thrand would go there. Somehow, that didn't stop him from imagining those soft lips on his.

"She wasn't my girlfriend," he said.

"Good," then she kissed his arm, patted his ass, and grabbed her bags. "Which way is my room?"

He pointed to the open door to the left of the living room. He realized, as she walked away with hips swaying, he was in big trouble.

He pulled off his hat, rubbed his head and the scruff on his face. So far, Cassie landing in his new hometown had been about as calm as a tornado touchdown. She was a nothing like the fourteen-year-old girl he had left behind. She had always been stubborn but never so straightforward and fearless. Nor had she been rockin' curves like that.

Her head poked around the corner of the door. "Bedlam, I'm hungry now."

He grinned at the nickname he hadn't heard in forever. "You got it, Buzzkill. You ready for the best BBQ this town has to offer?"

"Hell, yeah." Her playful innocent smile about did him in.

Thrand smirked as Cassie bit into a rib and moaned with satisfaction.

"You were right. This is amazing." She licked BBQ sauce off her fingers in blatant appreciation.

They were tucked against a window in the upstairs part of Buck's BBQ and sunlight turned her hair to spun gold. He couldn't take his eyes off her. Trying to merge the girl he'd left with the woman before him muddled his brain. There was nothing fancy about her. Just a woman with long, tanned legs, frayed shorts, black boots, and his baggy shirt. But she was like walking sunshine with all that hair and a mischievous smile.

"Glad you approve. Service sucks. But the food is incredible."

She laughed. "Service is always this bad?"

"Yup, but as you can tell, it's always packed."

"So you said you might have a job idea. Don't mean to rush it, but after this morning, I need a job. Quick."

"Sure. Jobs on the strip can be hard to get with all the people who come through this town, but I can pull some strings. You okay with serving liquor?"

Her left shoulder came up in a shrug and the wide neck of his shirt slipped, baring a little bit of skin.

"No problem. I just want to get paid." She turned her attention to the window and shook her head. "I've never seen so many people."

He glanced out the window at the crowd. "This is nothing. Wait until Friday and Saturday night. Traffic is backed up and you can barely maneuver up and down the sidewalks."

He hadn't thought it possible, but her face lit up even more.

"Really? I can't wait." Her attention went right back to the commotion out the window, a smile never leaving her face.

She tossed her napkin on the plate and abruptly stood. "Let's go. I want to see more."

Without waiting on him, she shoved back her chair and headed toward the exit. When she reached the stairs, she turned toward him, those green eyes sparkling. Her wavy hair trailed down her back and her lips curled up, teasing him. "Come on, Thrand."

Oh yeah...He was in trouble because she *was* trouble.

It was all he could do to keep up with her as she strode down the street, tossing question after question, barely letting him answer before the next one was out.

"Man, I wish I had my camera," she said in awe as they admired the 'Batman' building.

"Were you really into photography?" Hands in his pockets, he walked beside her. He had been in Nashville for years, so the new had worn off long ago. But seeing it through her eyes reminded him of how amazing this town was. How full of life.

"I guess. Got one at a garage sale for fun and realized..." She paused and studied the concrete. "Well, pictures are always there. They don't disappear."

She glanced up at him and he stopped in his tracks.

Pain flickered in her eyes before she turned away. It twisted up the ugly shame he had felt from the moment he had driven off. He'd disappeared on her. Without a word. He had tried to get her help but hadn't told her good-bye.

Before it could begin to fester, something else caught her eye. She captured his arm and pulled him along with a hundred more questions.

"You know, we don't have to see it all today. There will be more days," he said on a laugh.

She spun around, walked backwards and faced him. "Maybe. But maybe not."

He caught her hand to stop her from backing into someone and noticed the leather cuff. He stared at it knowing exactly who the cuff belonged to.

"Cameron," he murmured. His fingers grazed over the worn leather. He'd buried the hurt, the loss of his best friend...until now. Like a grisly wound that never really healed, she was slowly peeling off the scab.

Resignation settled on her face.

"One day, he was there. The next, he wasn't. Moments can't be wasted because you never know when it might be your last. I don't intend to lose another day. I've lost too many already." Her hand gripped his tightly. "I've missed too much. I've a lot to make up for."

There weren't any tears, only a sharp intensity with every word.

He shoved his glasses up and reached out to brush a thumb down her cheek. "You're right."

"So take me to my potential new job. I want to get my life started."

He flicked his glasses back down so she couldn't read the grief that swam just at the surface. "You got it, Buzzkill."

Without letting go of her hand, he led her down the street and around the corner to a place called Booseys Saloon.

Cassie could have stayed mad about being dependent on Thrand and the whole situation, but it wasn't in her. She'd shaken off the tension the moment she stepped on the bus, and promised herself she would just roll with it. Whatever happened, happened. She was here, not there, and that was good enough. Thrand had been a bonus she'd never imagined, but he wasn't what she remembered.

He used to be edgy. Restless. One could barely keep up with him. He'd come by the nickname, Bedlam, for a reason. He still had the swagger that made people get out of his way and turned every female head, but now, he seemed comfortable in his own skin. The younger Thrand was belligerent and in your face. Not anymore. He was more subdued. At ease. But then he had been free and able to figure it out.

But she didn't miss the anguish that crossed his face at the mention of Cam. He couldn't hide that from her even though he tried.

They stopped at a bar called Booseys.

She watched Thrand fist-bump a huge, scary-looking dude sitting on a stool at the entrance. The man wore black leather and had wild, long, curly, black and gray hair. It didn't help that he wore thick, heavy rings that would do some serious damage to anyone stupid enough to get in the way of his fists.

"Dooley, how's it going, my man?"

"Hey, hey Thrand. What's up?" Dooley turned his dark beady eyes on her. "What you got here? Jailbait?"

Thrand put his glasses on the back of his cap, his familiar grin in place once again.

"No, she's legal. Just barely, but legal." He winked at her, and she couldn't stop from smiling back. "This is Cassie, a friend from my hometown."

She extended her hand, and Dooley wrapped a surprisingly warm, soft hand around hers.

"Nice to meet you, missy. You should visit more often." Dooley chuckled as he looked her up and down, making her feel self-conscious. He leaned over to Thrand. "She got an older sister who wants to visit?"

"Sorry, man, you're outta luck. Hey, is Mick around?"

"Figures," he grunted. "Yeah, he's at the bar."

"Nice to meet you, Dooley." Cassie barely got out before Thrand took her hand and led her into the dimly lit interior. She would never tell him, but she loved the feel of his large calloused hand gripping hers.

The floors were worn hardwood and the walls were nothing but red brick lined with pictures of everyone from George Strait and Hank Williams, to Jason Aldean and Lynyrd Skynyrd. A bar ran almost the entire left side of the room and tables and chairs were set randomly throughout the place. A raised stage was in the back with a dancefloor in front of it.

"Hiya, Thrand," a pretty, very petite redhead said with a sweet southern drawl.

Cassie felt a lot like an Amazon standing next to the girl. She had to be almost a foot shorter than her and fifty pounds lighter.

"Hi, Lila. This is Cassie, a good friend of mine and, if luck holds, your new coworker."

She beamed. "Thrand, you are a godsend. Rachel's last day is Sunday."

"Buzzkill, it looks like your luck just turned around. I'll be right back." He patted her ass and walked toward the bar.

She blinked then laughed. She supposed she deserved that.

"Please tell me there is a story behind a nickname like Buzzkill because I'd smack the first jerk to call me that." Lila had her hand on her hip, bright blue eyes flashing.

Small she might be, but right then, Cassie knew the girl wouldn't take shit from anyone. "Thrand was best friends with my brother, Cameron. I used to follow and hang out with them when they jammed in the garage. I was just a kid and it didn't help with their efforts to hook up with girls. So he called me Buzzkill."

Lila burst out laughing and eyed her up and down. "He'd have to be a moron to call you that now."

She shrugged, heat filling her cheeks. "It's been seven years since he's seen me. I didn't even know he was here when I came to town."

Lila tilted her head and smirked. "And you just happened to run into him? In this town, bursting at the seams? That's almost too coincidental."

"You're telling me. Weird as hell," she muttered and glanced at Thrand, who was talking to some insanely tall guy behind the bar.

"Fate, baby girl, can be one strange bitch."

"Cassie," Thrand hollered and waved her over.

"Go. Tell Mick I'm getting you a shirt." She smiled and practically skipped to the back room.

She slid onto a barstool next to Thrand. He skated a hand under her hair and rested it at the nape of her neck. He used to do that from time to time back home. Then it was innocent. At least for him it was. For her? Not so much and her reaction hadn't changed a bit.

His hand sent a shock wave of awareness through her body. She tried to ignore the sensation as she was introduced to Mick, her new boss, who looked more like the leader of a biker gang, not the owner of a bar. He wore a black leather vest over a black shirt and his long, salt-and-pepper black hair was slicked back from his face. He sported a long, scraggly goatee and when he talked, she caught a glimpse of a gold tooth.

"Thrand said you'd been a waitress before?" Mick wiped out mugs.

She nodded. "Five years in a diner."

"You good on a busy night?"

Thrand's thumb brushed along the back of her neck lightly, almost absently, but she was hyper-aware of his every move. It made her skin hot and she shifted on her seat.

"Yeah, but small town diner busy, and Nashville busy, are probably two different things."

Mick laughed. "I like her, Thrand. No nonsense."

Thrand grinned, glanced at her, and instantly dropped his hand.

Her thinking was a lot clearer without his fingers doing a slow dance on her skin, but she'd choose his touch over clear thinking any day.

A woman walked up beside Mick and crooked an eyebrow. "I heard you hired a new girl without talking to me?"

Mick shrugged. "There she is."

Cassie sat up a little straighter when the lady's golden eyes landed on her. She felt like she was being measured or judged. She wasn't sure which.

"I'm Cassie."

"Dana. And you are how old?" She tilted her head, eyes narrowing.

"Twenty-one. As of yesterday." Cassie fiddled with her leather cuff.

She laughed. "Well, that explains the lost look."

Lila plopped on the stool beside her. "Here's your shirt."

Cassie held up the black shirt. Booseys was written in bold, jagged yellow and red font. But the neck was cut out wider, as were the short sleeves. She looked up at Dana, who was wearing the same shirt with sleeves and neck intact. "What happened to it?"

"Oh that. It's all about the tips, and if you show a lil' skin—" Lila shrugged as if that explained it all. "I know you're going to make a killing."

"I think she would do just fine without showing skin," Thrand muttered a frown marring his face.

"What fun would that be?" Lila giggled and hopped up to help some new customers.

"So this your girl, Thrand?" Dana asked. Humor danced in those odd-colored eyes as she glanced from him to Cassie.

He rubbed his chin and shook his head. "Just a friend from home."

"Sure. Cassie, you can start Monday at ten in the morning. That should give you some time to get used to the place before the crowd hits. We'll fill out all the paperwork then."

"Thanks, I really appreciate this."

"We'll just take it out of Thrand's hide if it doesn't work out." Mick grinned.

"You wish, old man." Thrand stood. "Ready, Buzzkill?"

When he held her hand as they walked out the door, her heart skipped a beat. It was hard to ignore all that Thrand had been to her when she was younger, even if he hadn't known about it.

He'd been her protector right alongside Cameron. They were her heroes. With those two looking out for her, she didn't have to worry about much. Except her dad.

Her worse fear...every time her dad made Cam pay for their mom's desertion. She'd left when Cassie was six and never looked back.

Cam made sure she didn't see much of the violence by locking her in a room or in a closet. It kept her from witnessing the blows but doors were thin, and she heard it all.

All the accusations.

Cussing.

Crashing.

Afterwards, she would see fresh holes in the walls and broken furniture. Worse were the bruises and cuts left on Cam.

She and Cam learned to stay away. Mostly in Thrand's garage. He was the only one who befriended them in a town full of hypocrites. As the boys got lost in their jamming, she got lost with them. And totally lost in Thrand.

They were the odd trio.

Until Cam died.

The way Thrand made her feel now was a lot like walking on a razor's edge. Confusing and tempting at the same time. He was all grown up and every inch the man she always thought he would be. Every time he looked her way, his crooked smirk appeared and the gray in his eyes darkened. That was all it took, and she was lost in him again.

He'd left her without a word, but it hadn't taken long and they'd picked up right where they had left off. The same banter and jokes they'd used back home. The only difference being, they were all grown up.

Soon they were back at his townhouse. She put her work shirt in her room, kicked off her worn, black, punk-style boots and padded back into the living room.

It was a nice place, although not large and surprisingly clean even though he was obviously a bachelor. A black leather couch sat in the living space with a recliner tucked into one corner. It was completely open to the kitchen, making it feel bigger than it was. Black granite countertops covered white cabinets and an island with three barstools separated the living room from the kitchen. A small table with two chairs rested against a wall.

Compared to where she'd been living, this place was lavish.

She looked up as he came downstairs and her breath caught. He wore a simple white tee and loose gym shorts. How he could make something so simple look so damn sexy was beyond her.

"Make yourself at home. You're welcome to anything in the fridge." He walked into the kitchen. "Would you like a beer?"

She smiled, repressed her instant attraction to him, and sat on a stool. "Sure, thanks. And if I didn't say it before, thanks for letting me stay here and for getting me a job. I'll try not to cramp your style."

He popped the top for her and placed the bottle on the island. "Glad to do it. And you won't."

She took a sip, then grinned. "After the Trina incident, are you sure?"

He laughed. "I guess that doesn't make me look that great, huh?"

"Guess I'll be your Buzzkill again. Be like old times."

Thrand's beer paused halfway to his lips. There was no way in hell she was a buzzkill. All that damn gold hair and those long legs...a man would have to be an idiot to not want to get wrapped up in them. He shook his head and did his best to remind himself she was off-limits.

"You showed up at a good time. Got the rest of the weekend off. I can show you around. And, Saturday, there's gonna be a bonfire outside of town, if you're interested."

She bit her lip, delight making her eyes sparkle. She was too damn cute for words.

"Yes. Whatever. I'm up for anything."

Thrand choked on his beer. He would *not* think about where his mind automatically went. It wasn't G rated and it definitely involved those long legs.

The next day, after they had lazed around all morning, laughing and talking about all the crazy shit he did back in the day, he asked, "Wanna see some sights?"

Her smile was his answer.

They walked into his garage, and she sucked in a breath.

"Holy shit, you got a Harley." Her eyes met his. "Please tell me you're taking me for a ride."

He was pretty sure he hadn't smiled this much in a long time. Her enthusiasm for life was contagious. "Of course. You ever ride one?"

She shook her head.

"You scared?"

She cut her eyes at him and put a hand on her hip. "Not even a little."

He should have known that her clinging to his back, her thighs pressed tight against his, would be a bad idea. He tried to concentrate on driving and not on the way she melded to him. After a few moments, he realized she wasn't holding on. He peeked back at her.

"Dammit Cas, hold onto me!" She'd been holding her arms out wide. Her head tilted back.

"But it's like flying." Her breath was hot on his ear as she set her chin on his shoulder and her arms tightened around his waist.

Trouble echoed in his head.

His pulse rocketed, and his body tensed. She was off-limits. It didn't matter she was grown up. It didn't matter he wanted to test the waters and find out exactly how sweet she tasted. And it sure as hell didn't matter that he had a good idea she wouldn't object. So he focused on the ride and not the girl.

The sky was blue and the air held a hint of summer. A perfect day for a ride and a stop at Centennial Park and the Parthenon. After he parked, she got off and turned in a slow circle, like she didn't know where to look first.

"It's so beautiful," she said, awe in her voice.

She was right. There were a lot of trees, a small lake and, of course, the Parthenon. He hadn't been here in a while, but he didn't have time to think about it, because she grabbed his hand and dragged him to everything she wanted to see. She was more enthusiastic than any kid he'd ever known.

Inside the museum, they admired the forty-two foot statue of Athena. Or rather, she did. He looked at her.

"Jiminy-cracker-jacks," she muttered.

He snickered. "You still say that?"

She pursed her lips and stuck out her tongue. "So what? Corny."

She took off, her laugh echoing through the building as he chased her out the door and caught her around the waist. He didn't even care that other visitors stared at them. He flung her over his shoulder as she squealed.

"You know I hate that, Buzz." He carried her outside.

"Corny Cornelius," she all but yelled and he smacked her on the ass. She kicked her feet in protest, shrieking with laughter the whole time.

Until he saw a security guard headed their way, a frown on the man's face.

Thrand put her on her feet and cleared his throat. "Sorry, sir. We're on our way."

Cassie was still giggling as he pulled her to a bench beneath a tree. She pushed her hair out of her face. Her cheeks were pink as she cut her gaze to him.

"It's sure good to see you, Cas."

She leaned into the crook of his shoulder and draped his arm over her, like she always used to do, and played with his hand. Her fingers traced patterns in his palm as she put her feet up on the bench. But she didn't answer him. Just looked out toward the scenery.

He put his chin on her head and inhaled a hint of citrus. She was the same but not. Her hand had done this so many times in years past, but now there was an awareness of every shift of her body that wasn't there before. Her light touch made his heart beat faster and ratcheted up his pulse. He couldn't stop imagining her silky hair against his naked skin.

"Your fingers are thicker than they were," she said. "More calloused. You play a lot more than you did."

"Have to when your livelihood depends on it."

Cassie considered him. "Pretty great you make a living doing what you love."

He met her gaze. "It sure is."

Looking down at her made his heart thump a little harder, and he had a difficult time remembering she was Cam's sister. When her lashes lowered and she bit her lower lip his thoughts screeched to a halt. He clenched his jaw. She would welcome his kiss. He saw it in the way her eyes slanted at him, the way her face flushed and the flutter of her pulse at her throat.

He pushed her up and stood.

"Hungry?"

"Sure," she replied, with a slight pout.

Thrand turned and motioned for her to follow. "I know a great burger place."

He had to get some space. There wasn't enough room in his head for the woman she was and the girl she had been.

There wasn't anything Cassie liked more than holding on to Thrand, but riding his motorcycle had to be a close second. It was thrilling and freeing and, as soon as she could, she vowed she'd get her own bike.

The wind rushed by making her feel alive. Free. The rumble of the engine vibrated through her body and she understood why people loved it so much.

They parked with a bunch of other bikes and she was mesmerized. One in particular caught her eye. An understated matte black Harley. She stopped to stare at it and slowly smiled.

Thrand stood beside her and smirked. "Like it, do you?"

"I'll own one of these some day."

He chuckled. "Really? Like the ride that much?"

She shoved at him playfully. "Damn right."

"I can see you on it. Come on."

He took her hand and a little thrill shot up her spine. She was pretty sure she would follow him just about anywhere when he laced his fingers with hers. Until she saw the sign of the burger place.

"Toad Suck Park Burgers? You can't be serious."

He turned so he was walking backwards, leading her in. He'd cocked his head, lips tugging up slightly, and she was right. She would follow him anywhere.

The place was decorated like a bad trailer park, complete with scarred cheap booths and plastic flamingos. The bar next-door had live music and was so loud they heard it clearly as the walls vibrated with the beat.

When the waitress plopped their baskets of burgers and fries on the table, the girl ignored her and smiled at Thrand. Good on him, he acted like he didn't notice.

She threw a fry at him. "Didn't want her number?"

He tossed a fry back at her and frowned. "Why would I want her number?"

"'Cause she would have given it to you." She laughed, then took a bite of a burger so big there was no way she would ever eat it all. "Oh, wow. This is really good."

"Told ya." He winked. "And no, she wouldn't."

"Right."

Her heart tripped as reality sank in. She never had to step foot inside her hometown again. Ever. And the man she'd missed as much as Cam was back in her life. It was surreal. Then he looked at her, and she had to keep herself from falling into those damn gray eyes.

"This place is so great," she said as much to him as to herself.

"Nothing like Woodbridge Grove."

"That's the best part about it." That was a lie. *He* was the best part about it. She didn't even bother trying to lie to herself. She was all about facing things head on, at least with herself. The man sitting across from her was who she'd dreamed about from a young age. Time hadn't erased that.

After dinner, they walked up and down Broadway. Every race and creed filled the sidewalks to bursting, and almost everyone wore cowboy boots. She pointed and laughed at what could only be described as a fifteen-person bar on a bicycle.

Everyone had to pedal to make it move, and it was hysterical watching it try to go uphill.

"I've ridden on one of those a few times," he said next to her ear. He stood behind her, his hand lightly touching her waist. "Almost impossible to get drunk on the thing."

"Oh, I gotta try that." She dashed to the nearest one.

Chapter 3

Thrand was hard-pressed to keep up with her as she wove her way through the crowd. They grabbed the last two spots on the pedal bar and rode down the street.

He was amazed. The girl he'd known never said much to anyone except him and Cam. This girl was the life of the party, laughing and talking to everyone. He didn't say much. Didn't have to. He was content to watch her. The sparkle in her eyes, the flash of her grin, the way she licked her lips when she downed a long drink of beer.

When they finally got off, she grinned ear to ear and flung her arms around him in a hug. Her body flush against his, he ceased to breathe.

"That was so much fun." Before he could register how her body fit to his, she had pulled back and turned away.

"Come on. Let's go there." She tugged and he stumbled blindly along as she fired off another round of questions—none that he had time to answer before she asked another one. Keeping up with her was like trying to grab a flame.

If he ever managed to, it would scorch him.

The sun blared through the window and made Thrand squint, but when his bed shifted, he frowned. On his stomach, he lifted his head to peer to the side. Perched on his bed, Cassie stared at him. A mischievous smile tugged at her lips as she snapped pictures of him with her phone.

"What are you doing?" He scrubbed at his eyes to clear his vision.

"Taking pictures." She clicked another one as he rolled and leaned on his elbow.

"Of me sleeping? Creepy much?"

Her lips quirked. "Probably. But you wouldn't wake up."

Cassie wore a tight tank top and tight pajama shorts. Her hair was a tangled mess, like she'd just woken up, and he had the insane urge to pull her to him.

"Do you always sleep naked?" She dropped her gaze and blushed.

"What the hell, Cas? Not only staring at me while I sleep but looking under the covers? Hold on. You didn't take pictures of me naked, did you?"

"I wouldn't do that."

Her flushed face didn't help her cause.

"Gimme that." He grabbed her phone and scanned through the pics. He was impressed. Only a cheesy camera phone, but she got some cool shots. Fortunately, he was decently covered.

"You need a real camera." He handed it back to her.

"I will when I get some money gathered up."

He watched her scan through the pics, a contented look on her face.

"Let's get you one."

Her green eyes widened. "I can't do that. I don't have any money and I won't let you do it. You've done enough for me already."

He brushed the tip of her nose with his finger. "Don't be silly. Let's call it a belated birthday present. Or, if it makes you feel better, you can pay me back later."

No way would he let her, but he would let her think so. He could tell by her grin and the way she was nearly bouncing in anticipation, she wouldn't be able to say no.

He slid out of bed. She squealed and covered her eyes. He laughed and looked over his shoulder in time to see her peeking through her fingers. "Nice try, Cas, but I can see you looking."

She covered her face again as he kicked the bathroom door shut. A part of him should feel guilty for giving her that little show, but she'd ogled his ass. Served her right.

Several hours later, they were headed home. He had his hand on the wheel as she took shots of him with the camera he'd just bought her. It gave him an odd sort of satisfaction to be able to buy something that gave her so much pleasure. She'd argued with him over the one he'd chosen. It was expensive, but he didn't care. He knew she'd never gotten much in her life, and he wanted to be the one to do it for her. He made enough to splurge now and then. It was worth it to see that glow of happiness on her face.

After getting home, he sat on the couch and plopped his feet up to get some chill time before heading to the bonfire later. The girl wore him out. She sat at the other end and curled her bare toes against his thigh as he turned on the TV.

"Thanks. I really don't know when I'll be able to pay you back."

"Nah, don't worry about it. You never know, you might be able to make some money with it."

"Never thought of that," she said.

"So you never told me what your plans were when you got to New York."

"I didn't have any plans. I was just going. Does it really matter?"

"You took off with no thoughts of what you were going to do when you got there?" Thrand couldn't imagine how hard that would be. Just up and go with only a small amount of cash and no idea of how you would survive once you got there.

She pursed her lips. "No. I had no idea. I was going to figure it out as I went. Isn't that what you did?"

He shook his head. "I had a lead here. I knew what I wanted to do."

She brows shot up in surprise then she lifted her chin. "I had to get out. It didn't matter what happened after that."

He dropped a hand to her foot and rubbed the arch. Her little toes flexed then curled. He studied her face. "Was it that bad?"

Cassie couldn't keep her eyes off him while his hand caressed her foot. Sparks shot through her and she kept imagining him this morning.

Lying on his stomach.

His broad, muscular back on wicked display.

It'd taken all she had not to reach out, touch him and run her fingers over his tattoos. When she noticed he wasn't wearing anything, she's taken a peek at his ass. What girl wouldn't? Then he stood. His entire body a feast for her eyes.

The sun's rays highlighted all the dips and planes of muscle. She'd been struck dumb. He looked better naked than with clothes. It was criminal. She did not need to think about that.

So she concentrated on his question...*was it that bad?*

How much did he really want to know? She opted for the truth. "Yeah. It was. At least until I moved out. It took a bit, but at least I don't have nightmares anymore."

Thrand paled and his hand stopped moving. "I'm sorry. I'm so damn sorry."

He dropped his head, and she really didn't know how to make him feel better.

"It is what it is. I'm free now. I've moved on." Her brows furrowed when he wouldn't meet her gaze. Surely he understood that shit happened and sometimes there wasn't anything to be done about it?

"Thrand." She poked him with her foot.

He raked a hand over his short hair in obvious agitation, then finally glanced at her.

"Life sucks, but it is what it is," she said.

"It shouldn't have been for you." He hopped up. "Going to the garage. Watch whatever you want."

She frowned at his departure. Did he blame himself for everything? She didn't see how he could. Hell, he'd been a kid, too, and his parents were asshats. She shook her head in confusion. She had to be misreading him because he had his life together.

"Cassie, get back down in the truck," Thrand yelled and tugged on her leg.

She stood in Thrand's seat, her torso up through the sunroof. Her arms spread wide and she hollered, loving how she could barely hear her own words. The wind lashed at her hair and left a tingle on her skin. The sky was slowly turning pink as the sun set. She closed her eyes and ignored Thrand.

She loved this feeling.

Free.

It was the most awesome thing in the world.

Then he swerved over and slammed it in park. "Get your ass back down, woman."

She slid in laughing. "That was awesome. I've always wanted to do that."

Windblown and alive, she inhaled his musky scent. He frowned at her and she was positive crawling into his lap would agitate him further. But that's exactly what she wanted to do.

"No more, okay?" Thrand pushed the button to slide the sunroof closed and put the truck in gear.

Cassie pouted, but didn't say anything and studied him. His jaw tensed, his strong hands tight on the wheel, she got the feeling she was the reason he was uptight.

They turned off the road, went through an open gate, and bounced across a rough pasture toward a circle of trucks with tailgates down. Thrand backed in next to a red pickup. A bonfire was lit in the center and Cassie couldn't keep the grin off her face, even if Thrand looked like he'd swallowed a bad apple.

They'd barely parked when a guy pulled open the driver side door.

"About time you got here. Why—" The guy stopped mid sentence when Cassie leaned forward. "Dammit, Thrand. You've been holding out on me."

She stifled a giggle. He appeared rumpled with sandy blond hair sticking up like he'd run his hand through it or just rolled out of bed. But he owned a lady-killer smile and light brown eyes.

Thrand was still trying to get his bearings from Cassie's revelations at the house. Just how bad had it been? He wasn't sure he wanted to know. Then she pulled that little stunt with the sunroof. His mood wasn't what you'd call great when he saw Ryan's face as he spotted Cassie.

"Ryan, this is Cassie. Cas, this is my best friend."

"Hi," she said, and waved before she scooted out her door.

He looked at Ryan. "Dude, you're gonna catch bugs with that thing."

Ryan's eyebrows shot up. "Where the hell did you find her?"

Thrand got out and leaned against the side of his truck. "Remember me telling you about Cameron?"

"Yup. Your high school buddy, right?"

"She's his sister."

Ryan whistled low. "She found you?"

"No. Coincidence, man." Thrand never talked about his hometown but, one night, on the anniversary of Cam's death, he'd drunk too much and spilled his guts to Ryan. He was the only person he'd ever told. "Ran into her on Broadway Wednesday night. She was headed to New York when her bus broke down."

"How long has it been since you've seen her?"

Thrand rubbed the back of his neck. "Seven years."

He dropped his hand and straightened when he spied Cas and Lila walking toward them. Cassie wore a loose tee that barely skimmed the top of her worn, low-rise jeans. Her golden hair slid past her shoulders in waves. So simple, but she had already gotten the attention of every male here.

He might have to kill somebody.

It wasn't long before someone had the music cranked, and red cups filled with alcohol were passed around. He knew everyone here, but he was a bit detached tonight.

Memories of the past echoed in his mind and the more he was around Cassie the more the present tangled with the past.

He was talking to a few of his buds, when the girls started a line dance. Something they always did, but all he saw was Cassie. The girl had moves that matched her curves. Sheer disregard for anything or anyone. Like no one watched or stared when *everyone* watched and stared. He grit his teeth while several guys took turns dancing with her.

After guy seven—yes, he was fucking counting—Thrand's patience snapped. He glared at guy eight who thought he was next. Thrand took her free hand and spun her. She gasped, then grinned up at him as he moved her into a two-step, dust kicking up around them.

"Having fun?" he asked.

"You know I am." She scooted in closer when a slow song hit the radio.

With his hands on her waist—he didn't dare move them lower—he kept space between them. "Bonfires suit you."

They did. A little too well. Her tanned skin and golden hair glowed in the light of the orange flame.

"Really? This is my first one." She clasped her hands casually behind his neck.

"Let me guess. You've always wanted to go to one?"

She wrinkled her nose at him. "How'd you know?"

"I'm seeing a pattern." He barely resisted kissing her. She was so fucking cute when she did that. But everything she did stirred his blood in a way that no other girl ever had. She inhaled life at warp speed and he was learning quick, this girl didn't hold back. She drew him in like a moth to flame.

When the song changed, Lila grabbed her arm and dragged her off for more line dancing. This time, Ryan joined the group of girls, making them laugh. Thrand propped a hip against his tailgate and nursed a beer, that's when Trina walked up to him.

He glanced at her but didn't say anything. He didn't want to talk to her and had no intention of doing so.

"So how long is this gonna last?" Her high-pitched voice had him cringing.

He sighed and closed his eyes briefly. Why could this girl not get the hint? He turned to her. "Should I pretend to know what you're talking about?"

"You knew I would be here. Just rubbing my face in it?"

"I don't have any idea what you're talking about. And no, I didn't know you'd be here, nor did I care. Lady, you don't fuck some guy you just met and expect more than *just* that." He hated being so blunt, but damn, he was tired of her shit. She reared back her hand to slap him, but Cassie shoved the girl to the ground before it hit.

"Don't you dare touch him," Cassie yelled.

Thrand was so shocked all he could do was stare.

Trina shrieked and came after Cassie with her nails but Cassie slugged her, knocking her to the ground. It was obvious who knew how to fight. Thrand encircled Cassie's waist when it looked like she wasn't finished. All Trina did was lie in the dirt and cry.

"Whoa, tiger. I think you made your point."

Cassie's eyes flashed in a way he recognized. It never boded well. She jerked out of his arms and stomped off away from the fire. He shoved his drink into Ryan's hand and took off after her.

"Cassie." Thrand reached for her arm and she whirled around. Cameron and Cassie's eyes matched and it was like seeing Cam all over again. That angry fire all the same.

She gripped his shirt and pulled him in close. Her stare hot. "Tell me she was only a one night stand."

His body reacted instantly to hers, which made his voice nothing but air. "You know it was."

She nodded, stepped back and released him. Her lips twitched. "I've always wanted to do that. Fight for someone I cared about."

"Glad I could be of assistance." Unlike Cam, Cassie's anger disappeared in a flash and it left him floundering, trying to keep up with her moods.

She was about to walk away when she swiveled around, stepped up to him and put her fingers on his lips.

He clenched his hands to keep them to himself. She tilted her head, leaned up on tiptoes, and touched her lips to his. So brief he might have imagined it, except her nails raked down the front of his shirt before she skipped off back to the party.

His body on fire from her nearness, he struggled for air. She wound him up so tight he couldn't think straight. His mind whirled with everything he shouldn't be thinking about that girl.

Cam's sister...Cam's sister.

Maybe, if he repeated it enough, he'd keep his senses from scattering. Her distant laughter tickled his oversensitive nerves. He could pick her voice out of the chatter and he rubbed his neck. She'd only been here a few days and his world had been turned upside-down.

It was several minutes before he was able to make his way toward the bonfire. He needed to get his emotions, and libido, under control first.

The rest of the party passed without incident. Most of the guys got the hint and kept their distance from Cassie. He knew he was being an ass and probably growling at every male who got near her. It was all fucked up because she wasn't his.

Knew she *couldn't* be his.

That realization didn't stop his over protectiveness but she didn't seem to care. Matter of fact, she made a point of touching him every time she got close. Casual, but oh-so-nerve-wracking to his internal battle.

Several hours later, they packed up to leave.

On the way home, silence reigned. Her head was in his lap with one foot on the floorboard, the other on the seat. Her green eyes stared up at him only a few moments before she'd fallen asleep.

Unable to resist, he slid his hand into her silky hair. Her contented sigh made him leave it there. He was so tied up in thoughts of her, Cam and the past, he couldn't remember how he'd gotten to his driveway.

For the second time since he'd run into her four days ago, he carried her into his house. He laid her in her bed, pulled off her boots, and covered her up. He didn't trust himself to do more.

He watched her curl a hand under her chin. That glimpse of innocence he'd seen before was back. Totally relaxed, she reminded him of the kid he'd left. But only partially. Those lips were too full. She'd proved that when they had grazed his earlier tonight. The curves under the blankets belonged to a woman.

He turned and left before his thoughts ran away with him and he tested just how far she would let him go.

Cassie woke, then winced as she looked at her hand. It was a bit sore as she flexed her bruised knuckles but it had been so worth it. Too bad Thrand stopped her. She would've loved to finish what the bitch had started.

She licked her lips, recalled the taste of beer on his and the way his body moved as they danced. She sighed and stretched. She didn't regret a single thing that had happened so far.

She rolled out of bed and took a long, hot shower. It was one of her favorite things and it helped her relax. At least it usually did. This morning, her mind was too wrapped up in what Thrand might be thinking. Would he still be tense?

They spent the day around the house, and she couldn't help but notice he was quiet. And definitely tense. He didn't have a lot to say and made sure they didn't touch. At all. Honestly, it amused her. She knew she was a lot different than he remembered. Every once in a while, she would catch him staring at her as though he couldn't figure her out. Other times, his eyes were dark, giving her a good idea what was on his mind.

They were sitting at the island, eating grilled burgers that evening when she asked, "Anything I need to know about Boosey's before my first day tomorrow?"

He shrugged. "Not really. Dana and Mick are a couple. Angel is their kid. She works the bar, too. Mick is pretty protective of his girls, so if you have trouble, let him know."

"Good to know."

"Where did you learn to fight?" His expression was wary as he asked.

She dropped her chip and peered up at him. "Necessity."

"Fuck." He shoved off the stool and paced into the living room.

She frowned. "Cam showed me a few moves before he died. For just in case. You had to know I would need it."

His fists clenched. "There is no way you could fight Willie."

She snorted. "You're right. I avoided my old man at all costs. I fought the kids at school."

That brought him up short.

"Stop thinking you could have protected me from everything. While you guys were in school with me, yeah. It helped. But even if y'all had been around after you graduated, it wouldn't have stopped most of it."

He grimaced and narrowed his eyes.

"Everyone in that town was trash, but I was on the bottom rung. You know that. They took stuff out on me." She shrugged. "It came in handy last night."

"Last night wasn't necessary." He shot a glare at her then rubbed between his eyes. "I'm glad you got out of that shit-hole."

"Me, too."

He sat on the couch and flipped through channels when Cassie went to her room to get her camera. The drum set that took up most the space in the bedroom caught her attention. She bit the inside of her cheek, remembering how he banged on those drums, how lost he would get in his music, and how enthralled she would get.

She wanted to hear him play.

Needed it.

Her body tingled in anticipation of the rush his playing gave her. Years couldn't erase the memory.

She spun around and headed back into the living room.

"Thrand, play me something."

Chapter 4

Thrand considered her as she stood beside the couch. He wasn't shocked by her request but by her demeanor. He caught a flash of the girl who used to ask him to play in just the same way. Eager, yet hesitant and shy.

"Sure. What do you want to hear?" He got up, then stilled. Her smile lit up the room.

If she smiled like that every time he told her yes, there was no way in hell he would ever tell her no.

"You know which one."

Of course. He should have known. She'd always asked him to play that old 90's metal tune.

"You got it, Buzzkill."

He sat behind the kit and knocked his sticks together three times before he hit the first note. He usually got lost playing this song. So many memories of him and Cam rocking it out. But this time, he was more interested in the girl sitting on the bed, her eyes bright with anticipation.

It wasn't long before she stood on the bed, belting out the chorus. Her blond hair flew as she jammed. Blood pumped hotly through his veins and sweat slid down his spine as he watched her total abandon.

Shy and hesitant was gone.

Trouble was back.

After the wild song, the quiet was almost deafening. She fell back on the bed. Her chest rose and fell with her rapid breaths. But she grinned from ear to ear, and she laughed as she sat up and focused on him.

"Damn. I missed hearing you play that." She shoved hair out of her face and walked to him, a gleam in her eye. She scooted herself between him and the snare, and straddled his lap.

He went still, sticks frozen in his hand.

"Cas," he muttered, words barely choked out. "What the hell are you doing?"

She slid her arms around his neck, her fingers curling into his nape. Only inches separated their bodies.

She leaned in and her breath tickled his ear. "Do you really have to ask?"

It was like a head-on collision when her lips branded skin right below his ear. Desperately, he grasped for reason, some way to stop this disaster.

"You're Cameron's kid sister," he whispered before she moved a hair's breath away from his lips.

"Yes." Her green gaze bored into his. "And I want to kiss you."

One touch of her lips on his and he was gone. She tasted of heaven, sweet and pure. He dropped his sticks and wound his hands into her mass of silken hair. She bit at his lips, and he tilted her head so he could delve deeper. Her groan of appreciation had him slipping further under her spell.

She gripped his shoulders then pushed off his hat and scraped through his short hair while he kissed down her neck. He wanted—no needed—her closer. As though she read his mind, she arched her body into his. Seared and marked him like a hot iron.

Her hips ground into him...searching. He cupped her ass and pulled her in.

Her yes was drawn out into the sexiest sound he'd ever heard. Her nails slid under the neck of his tee, leaving marks as she rocked against him.

He was lost in the way she moved and clung to him. Hands on her hips, he helped her grind into him. Her full breasts flat against his chest, he nipped at her neck. Her hips rolled, just like she had last night while dancing, making him harder than he already was. He wanted this girl.

Naked and writhing under him.

She grabbed his head and crushed her lips to his. Her tongue swept along his and her little pants let him know just how close she was to the edge. He wanted her over that fucking edge. He shoved his hand up her shirt. Under her bra. Her skin hot beneath his hand as she flung her head back.

"Thrand," she moaned and shuddered in his arms.

Shock rippled through his head.

Oh, hell.

He had just gotten Cameron's little sister off.

He jerked his hand out from under her shirt just as those heavy lidded eyes landed on him. It took all his self-control to think and not feel.

"Cassie. We have to stop." He gripped her shoulders to push her back.

She blinked and grimaced. "What?"

"We can't do this." Guilt ate at his gut, because when he looked at her, he didn't see Cam's little sister. He saw a woman who was ready to take on the world.

And him.

She pursed her lips, and it was all he could do to not capture them again. Hastily, he pushed off the drum stool and backed up, stopping only when he hit the wall.

"I'm not fourteen anymore, Thrand." Anger laced her words. "And you damn sure noticed that."

"I know." Like he didn't notice how well her breast fit in his hand. "But you're not just some chic. You're Cam's sister and my friend. Do you know how bad things like this can fuck up a friendship?"

Her eyes widened and she stood, hands on her hips. "It's been seven years. Seven. With no word from you. Nothing. Friends don't disappear like that."

"And I regret it. There hasn't been a day that has gone by that I haven't thought of you and Cameron. I have no excuse for not checking up on you, but..." He didn't know how to tell her how ashamed he had been—and still was—for leaving like that. It was a thorn that pierced him, day in and day out.

She threw it in his face. And he deserved it... every bit of it.

"You thought about me but didn't check up on me?" She grabbed his sticks and threw them against the wall. "You know, I get why you left. I do. Why would anyone want to stay in that hellhole if they could get out? But then, nothing."

"You don't understand. I tried to get you help, and your dad threatened me with statutory rape for trying to intervene. Social services said they would take care of it but told me, in no uncertain terms, that if I didn't butt out, I would end up in jail. Then I found all my stuff piled in my parents' driveway after they'd heard I was involved with trying to help you. There wasn't much I could do." The shame and guilt of it all came pouring out. It had eaten at him for seven long years, and even if he couldn't fix it, he could at least try to explain. "I left without a word because I knew you would ask me to stay, and I've never been able to tell you no. But I couldn't stay."

Tears shimmered in her eyes as she slid back onto his drum stool.

"You're the one who got social services involved? Hell, I should have put two-and-two together when you were gone shortly after." She shook her head, disbelief on her face. "My dad told me you left because everyone always leaves me. Because I was nothing but trash. If my mother didn't want me, why would anyone else?"

Outrage and grief choked him. "You know that isn't true."

"I didn't want to think so, but..." She shrugged. "You never sent word. Nothing. Cam was gone. My mother left when I was six. Everyone left."

The vacant look in her eyes carved the hole in his heart deeper. There was nothing he could say to make it better.

"Did they help you? They said they would." He hoped liked hell they had.

She angrily wiped at the one lone tear.

"Oh, yeah. They got involved. At first I was relieved, then I realized they were going to put me in a foster home." Her jaw worked and nostrils flared. "So I lied. Told them it was fine. Made the house look presentable for their visits. It may have been hell, but at least it was a hell I knew."

Thrand sagged against the wall. He couldn't believe it. He'd hoped and prayed that she'd been okay. But he knew what Cam had lived with. Cassie had not been fine. It left a sour taste in his mouth and his chest tightened. There was no way he would ever be able to apologize for leaving her like that. "I'm so sorry, Cassie."

"You tried. Which is more than anyone, other than Cam, had ever done. It's fine though. Doesn't matter anymore. I got out. I don't know if it was luck or fate that I ran into you, but I would have been fine one way or another. I appreciate the help, but I don't want or need a hero."

She stood and strode toward him, her hand fiddling with the leather cuff. "I kissed you because I wanted to. You could have had more, but your so-called morals stopped you. One day, you might regret it. Life is too uncertain to waste on 'what ifs.'"

Then she stormed out, the front door banging shut.

Had a truck hit him, he couldn't have felt more fractured. That girl ripped out his heart even though it thundered in his chest. He hung his head and stared at the floor, the sticks not far from his feet. She hadn't aimed at him, but he might have felt better if she had. Because she was right. On all counts.

He might be five years older than her, but she understood more about life than he could ever claim. He scrubbed his face with his hand and swallowed bitter rage. He had seen the scars on Cam. He'd seen just how fucked up Cam had been. How had Cassie even survived it?

Chapter 5

Tears spilled over her cheeks as Cassie ran down the concrete steps in bare feet. The air was cool, but she didn't care. She took off at a fast clip down the paved street. No way could she stay in there and let Thrand see her cry. She'd been so caught up in his music. The rush of want that made her blood pump. The need in his darkened eyes. She'd made the first move, knowing he wouldn't.

His greedy hands and scorching kisses told her he wanted her. And lord he could kiss. Her dreams couldn't compare to the reality of his lips on hers or those strong arms that held her while she came apart.

She wanted him.

Always had.

She didn't let him know how devastated she'd been when he'd disappeared. She'd even gone to his home, only to have his parents slam the door in her face and then put a restraining order on her. She couldn't even serve them when they'd come into Ruth & Pops.

She might have been only fourteen, but her feelings for him had been real. Were real. Seeing him again reminded her how much in love with the stubborn ass she had been and, to her utter surprise, still was. She had no idea he'd tried to save her. Had no idea that he'd been driven from her. That only solidified it.

She was here. He was here.

There was no way she would miss her chance. Not again. He may have shut her down, but this wasn't over. She had no delusions that this was a forever thing. This wasn't a fairy tale. Had never believed in them anyway.

She knew for a fact Thrand Medlam wanted her and she might only get him for a little while...but she would have him.

She furiously wiped at her tears as a steady rain fell. *Of course.* She balled up her fists and screamed at the sky. If fate was involved maybe it should take a long hike down a short plank. She was having a hard enough time without that evil bitch stirring the pot.

It was about that time she heard shoes slapping on the wet pavement.

"Cassie, come in out of the rain."

She sighed when she heard his strained voice and turned. It figured. Thrand looked even better under the dim streetlights with his shirt plastered to his body. Dammit.

"Yeah, I'm coming," she muttered and stomped off ahead of him.

She didn't stop when she got inside, just went straight to her room without a word. She might be in love with him, but she wasn't a simpering fool.

Thrand was gone when Cassie got up the next morning, but at least he'd left a note.

"Working in studio today. Take the truck. ~ T"

Keys were lying next to the scrap of paper. She grabbed the keys as she walked out the door to her new job.

The first thing she noticed at Booseys was Dooley wasn't on door duty. She stepped inside and realized the place was very dead. No band in sight, just music playing from the speakers overhead and a couple of people sitting at the tables.

She walked up to the bar, where a slender girl worked. Chin-length, straight, black hair framed a surprisingly angelic face, with storm-blue eyes that matched Mick's.

"You must be Cassie," the girl said softly. "I'm Angel."

"Nice to meet you. Mick's daughter, right?"

"I am." She handed her an apron. "Just keep the place clean, and take orders as they come in. It will pick up in a couple of hours and Lila will be in a bit."

Several hours later, Cassie was leaning against the bar for a short break, amazed at how busy the place had gotten even though they kept telling her it was still slow.

She tightened her ponytail and glanced up when Mick made his way toward her. "Holding up okay, Jailbait?"

She laughed at the name. "Dooley?"

"Yup. That's all the man would call you, so looks like you're stuck with it."

"I'm okay. It's just light years from the diner."

"You're doing good. No worries. The customers like you. All I care about. You'll get used to the crowd. You have any questions or problems just let me or Dana know." Mick tossed her a wink and walked off.

A band was setting up when one of the members approached her.

"Cassie," Ryan gave her a slight hug. "Didn't know you worked here."

She hugged him back. His carefree attitude was infectious and it was impossible not to like him. She placed tumblers on a tray. "Today is my first day. I didn't know you played."

"Guitar."

"Sweet. Is that your band?"

"Naw. Just filling in." In the daylight, his eyes were a pretty shade of cinnamon brown, but he still had that playful grin, and he was just as disheveled-looking. He made her want to ruffle his hair.

When she felt eyes on her, she looked up in time to see Thrand walk through the door. Her breath seized. He wore his signature black cap on backwards and had that swagger that she knew so well. It hadn't been that long since she'd seen him, but in the light of day, all she could focus on was his lips and how they had made her feel the night before.

He didn't stop until he was right in front of her. "Hey, Cas. Ryan."

Cassie didn't say anything, just smiled. Not that she would know what to say anyway.

"Hey, man. How'd studio go today?" Ryan asked.

"Went all right." Thrand leaned in a little closer. He cocked his head toward the rest of the band. "You know you're better than that?"

"I like playing live." Ryan shrugged.

Thrand snorted. "To get the girls."

Ryan winked at her and grinned. "Of course. Why else?"

"Of course," Cassie added, enjoying the banter between the two.

Thrand slapped Ryan on the back and turned those intense gray eyes on her. "Ryan is a damn good guitar player and fair singer."

"Fair? Dude, that's all you're giving me?"

Thrand's laugh was a deep chuckle that left goose bumps on her skin. "Sorry, man. All you're getting."

"Not everyone can be as good as you."

"While you boys argue over who's better, I should get back to work. Good luck with the girls, Ryan." She returned his wink and grabbed another empty glass on the way to the bar.

Chapter 6

As Cassie walked off, Thrand's muscles tensed, ready to demand Lila give her a new shirt. The one Lila had altered for her slipped completely off one shoulder and the bottom was just a ragged edge, giving a glimpse of tanned flesh. Her honeyed locks were pulled up in a ponytail, wispy bangs hung slightly in her eyes. All it did was bring out those greens that landed on him now and then while she worked.

"Like that, huh?"

"What?" Thrand looked at Ryan, confused.

"Dude, I saw you with her Saturday night, remember? You might want to change the 'friend' term when you introduce her to people."

"What the hell are you talking about?" Thrand was still so wrapped up in what happened last night he was having trouble following anything. Even his drum work had been off today.

"It doesn't matter who she was. Cam's sister or not, if you feel like that, you need to do something about it. A girl like that won't be alone long."

"It does matter that she's Cam's sister. And she's just a friend," Thrand said, not wanting to think about her hooking up with someone else.

"Only if you're sure." Ryan went back to setting up.

Thrand moved to the bar and sat down.

Angel came over and put a beer in front of him.

"Thanks," he said absently, as he pried his eyes away from Cas to look at Angel who was glaring at him.

"All this time, the other girls never bothered me 'cause I knew all I had to do was wait. But she's the one." Tears brimmed in the girl's eyes but didn't fall.

Thrand opened his mouth, but he wasn't sure what to say.

"She's just a friend," he muttered. Was he trying to convince himself at this point?

"No, Thrand. I'm *just* a friend. Figure out the difference." She fled toward the back room, leaving him staring after her, wondering what the hell he'd done.

It wasn't two seconds before Mick was there, glaring at him. "Anything you need to tell me?"

Thrand lowered his beer and sighed. Sure, he'd talked to Angel, a lot he realized. But he'd never seen her as anything other than a friend. Just a nice girl...who had paid *a lot* of attention to him. Knew his favorite beer. Had even chipped in advice when he'd been working on lyrics while at the bar. They'd never dated but they had gone for coffee.

Ah, fuck.

"No, Mick. I would never do that. You know that." He rubbed at his chin and shook his head. "I had no idea—"

Mick held up his hand. "I didn't think you did but had to double-check. Angel is back there, throwing out the trash and cussing you a blue streak. Not really like her."

How many times today would he be struck dumb? "Honestly, I had no clue."

Mick smirked as he grabbed a few beers for customers. "You were the only clueless one."

That was about all he could take. He got up and walked out the door without looking back.

When Cassie stepped through the door, furious drumming echoed through the house. She dropped the keys on the kitchen counter, sauntered to her room and leaned against the doorframe to watch Thrand pound away.

Shirtless, his muscles strained and accentuated the full tattooed sleeve on his left arm. The sound was deafening in the tiny room. His eyes were closed, and sweat dripped off him like he had been at it for a while.

Her heart pounded. The anger he poured into his kit was as frightening as it was enticing. She wasn't sure what had made him so furious, but she couldn't look away. So oblivious and lost in his own world, he sucked her in with it.

He stopped suddenly and stared at her.

Oh hell. He was mad at *her*.

She swallowed hard and clenched her hands, waiting for the hateful words she knew had to be coming. Although she had no idea what she'd done.

He tossed his sticks and stalked toward her. She backed up against the doorframe and clung to it. She wasn't short, but with him breathing heavy, his eyes almost black with rage, he towered over her. She lifted her chin and stared right back. No way in hell would she cower.

"You," he said and pointed at her. "It's all your fault. Turning my world upside down in only five fucking days. I was happy. Content with what I was doing, where I was. Then you waltz in and rip it all apart."

Her fingers dug into the doorframe for support and tears strangled her. He was going to throw her out, and she had nowhere to go.

He rubbed his head and dropped his arms, fury glittering in his darkened gaze. "I didn't get a fucking wink of sleep last night. All I could think about was you and your damn green eyes. Your words that dug up all the shit I wanted to leave buried."

"Fine. I'm sorry. I'll leave," she said.

"You think it's that easy? That you can walk out as quickly as you came in and everything will fall back into place?" He laughed bitterly. "I'll always be haunted by whatever your dad did to you. And I'll never be able to wipe from my mind what I did to Cam's little sister."

Stunned, Cassie shoved his sweaty chest, which was so close—too close—to her.

"I'm not *just* Cameron's little sister, and we didn't do a damn thing." Enraged, she pushed him again so he backed against the door. "I'm Cassie Rose Dalton, a grown woman who has lived through hell to get to this point. You better get that through your thick skull, Thrand Cornelius Medlam. If you can't recognize that, then that's your problem. And your loss."

He said nothing. Just stood there with a dazed expression. She wanted to shake him. Kiss him senseless. Force him to admit she was right. She was more than what he refused to see.

Then the fucking doorbell rang. She spun on her heel, picked up the keys, and flung open the door.

Ryan's smile disappeared when she scowled at him.

On impulse, she grabbed his head and kissed him with every ounce of anger she possessed. Then, just as quickly, she thrust him away and stalked out the door. Tears blurred her eyes as she wiped at her lips. The only lips she wanted were Thrand's.

"What the hell—" Cassie heard Ryan mutter right before she fired up Thrand's truck and peeled out of the driveway.

Cassie sat at a corner table in Booseys. A few shots of whiskey did nothing to wipe out the words Thrand had so carelessly tossed at her. She was waiting for Lila to get off because she didn't have anyone else to talk to, and she was tipsy enough to need someone.

What she really needed was a new place to stay, but with very limited funds, her choices were nil. She could ask Lila, and would if it came down to it, but even she knew she didn't *really* want to leave Thrand's house. She knew where she wanted to be, but she had to be wanted in return.

Lila fell into a chair beside her. "All right girlfriend, what's going on? You look like someone just shot your dog."

She sulked at the petite redhead and puzzled on where to start. She opened her mouth several times before anything would come out.

"Thrand only sees me as his best friend's kid sister. I'm more than that. I know he knows it, but right now, denial is his mantra. I didn't get free of that hell I was in just to be pigeonholed into some role that doesn't exist anymore." She dropped her head to the table on a groan. "Why the hell did

I get stranded here? And to have him, of all people, end up saving my ass? I wish I'd never seen him again."

Lila snorted. "Really? I don't believe that for a minute."

"You can't be serious. This is a mess. It's just my continued bad luck that I run into him after finally being free."

"So? Then you would never have known for sure."

Cassie lifted her head and peeked at her. How had she figured her out so quick?

"Have you banged him yet?" Lila asked all matter of fact.

Cassie would have thought it funny, except for last night.

"No. Not for lack of trying, though." She picked up her whiskey glass, realized it was empty, then set it back down. "I'd say he's made it clear that he doesn't want me, but that's not true. His eyes say one thing, his lips say another, and his words say something totally different."

Lila leaned forward, her blue eyes spooky bright. "Tell me something. If you walked away right now, would you always wonder?"

Would she? Hadn't she told him life was too short not to take in everything—because you never knew when your number would be up? Hadn't she promised herself just last night that she would have him one way or another? Regardless of the outcome, she wanted to know the end result.

So she'd landed in the same town as Thrand. She had no clue why or how it happened, but she would regret it if she didn't see this through. Life was a clusterfuck maze. There wasn't a crystal ball or fairy godmother to tell her what to do. All she had was instinct. And instinct told her to go after what she wanted.

She lifted her head, determination steeling her.

Lila's freckled cheeks broke out into a knowing smile. "Then make him see you. As a woman, and not the girl he knew."

Cassie took a breath and nodded. "You're right."

"There's my girl." Lila's grin spoke volumes as she patted Cassie's hand and hopped up. "I'll see you later, sweetie. I've got an appointment at the nail salon."

She waggled her fingertips and headed out the door.

It wasn't long before Cassie was tired of the crowd, so she wandered outside and down the sidewalk. She hadn't seen the Cumberland River at night yet, so she ambled toward its edge. She propped her arms against the railing and stared across the wide expanse. From here, she could see LP Field and the metal art statue called Ghost Ballet, which she thought looked more like parts of a suspended roller coaster.

Here it was quiet with the noise of Honky Tonk Row behind her. The water flowing down the banks soothed her and the lights of Nashville reflected off the calm ripples. Not many people were taking in the peaceful setting, but she needed to clear her head.

She loved Thrand. She knew it like she knew her heart thumped harder when she was around him. She wasn't in the habit of lying to herself. Lila was right. She couldn't let him slip through her fingers so easily. What about their friendship? Could she even consider them friends anymore? So many years had passed without contact. Combine that with the heat in his eyes and none of it screamed friend. There was a whole lot more there than that. But what if all went bad? Where would that leave her?

A chill slithered up her spine.

She looked at the night sky as she rubbed the leather cuff that had once belonged to her brother and took a deep breath.

"Cam, I don't know what to do."

He didn't answer. He never did when she talked to him.

But it made him feel not so far away.

Thrand was going to take off after Cassie, but then she'd kissed Ryan. That had stopped him in his tracks. The squeal of tires let him know how pissed off she was.

He'd waited up for her. Sitting in a recliner stuffed into the corner of his living room. In the dark. What was she doing? Who she was doing it with? None of it was his business. He gripped the arms of his chair tighter and knew, without a doubt, he wanted to make her his business.

A war raged within him.

She'd woken that part of him he'd put to rest...Bedlam. Known for taking what he wanted and asking later. He tapped the arm of his chair as Cam's face came to mind. The only thing Thrand should be doing is protecting Cassie and helping her get on her feet.

Not pinning her to the wall and claiming her.

He glanced up when he heard the click of the door. She never turned on a light so she didn't see him as she went straight to her room.

He took a relaxing breath, got up, and went to his room.

She was safe.

The next few weeks passed in a blur and Thrand avoided her when he could. But living together and barely talking was getting old. He honestly didn't know what to say to her. Every time their paths crossed, all he could do was stare and remember her in his lap. His neck would sizzle just like the brand he swore she'd laid on him.

She didn't bother to hide the fact she wanted him. Her eyes said it all. He would catch her walking around his house singing some song off the radio in nothing but boy shorts and a tight tank. Her bras were always hanging on his towel bar and, more than once, he'd found her clothes and panties mixed in with his laundry.

He was on edge, and the only way he could release it was to bang the hell out of his drums. Studio time used to be enough, but it was too tame. He needed something harder. So he had lined up a few gigs to work, even though he had been busy at the studio.

He pulled his Harley into the garage and noticed his truck was parked in the drive, along with Ryan's motorcycle.

He walked in through the back door to the sound of their laughter and the strong smell of marijuana.

They sat on the floor, passing a joint between them.

"What the hell?" Thrand demanded and saw red. It was one thing for Cassie to have kissed Ryan when she was mad, but had something come of it? He glared at Ryan.

"Dude, chill. Not what you think," Ryan said but was laughing as he said it.

"Why are you getting high in my living room?" He wanted to add, *and alone with Cassie.*

She was smiling, her eyes a bit glassy. "I wanted to try it."

"You wanted to try it?" He arched a brow at Ryan and crossed his arms over his chest. "And you just happened to have some on you?"

Ryan shrugged. "I came to see you. You weren't here, and Cassie and I got to talking. Somehow it came up that she had never tried it. So, I helped."

"Of course you helped."

Thrand was at a loss. Cassie was reckless and hell-bent on driving him mad. She sat on the floor, legs crossed, with her head leaned back against the couch. Her hair looked like gold spread out over the black leather.

She licked her lips and smiled. "Ryan's a good friend. He's helping."

He turned an eye on Ryan who wasn't as high as he first seemed.

"Hey guys, I gotta split." Ryan climbed to his feet.

"Awww, but we were just getting started," Cassie said with a sulk. "He was telling me all about your crazy conquests."

Ryan coughed. "Yeah, sorry, Cas. Maybe another time."

Faster than Thrand thought possible, Ryan was out the door.

Thrand sat on the couch beside Cassie and couldn't take his eyes off her. "Do you really have to try everything? Is there any line you won't cross?"

She pursed her lips while she pondered the ceiling before her gaze settled on him. "There might be, but I haven't found one yet."

"I was afraid you might say that." Exactly what he didn't want to hear.

"Thrand, do you want me gone?" A trace of sadness lingered in her eyes.

"What?" He shook his head. "No."

"You avoid me. You don't talk to me. It's like I'm in your way."

All true. He sighed and slid to the floor so they were eye level. "I'm sorry. I've been an ass, haven't I?"

"Yes." Then she scooted up against him and snuggled into the crook of his arm.

He had no choice but to wrap an arm around her.

"I missed you," she said softly against his shirt.

He knew she wasn't just talking about recently. He kissed the top of her head, the silkiness of her hair brushing against his lips. "I missed you, too."

"Can we please talk?" Her arm lay carelessly across his waist. "I don't like all this silence. You used to talk to me."

There was a time when they would talk about anything and everything. But it was so long ago. He'd gotten a glimpse of that those first few days she was here, but then she'd kissed him. That had changed everything. He wanted the easy companionship they had before, but every time he looked at her, all he felt was her lips on his. He was all twisted up and he had no idea what to do with any of it. Guilt, mixed with this insane attraction, was driving him out of his mind. He couldn't make peace with it.

She turned her head up toward his and he met her gaze. High cheekbones, full lips and green eyes tempted him. He tried to not want to kiss her. But those lips were right there. Had their first kiss been a fluke? Had he just imagined that intense feeling? His heart hammered in his chest, he tightened his arm around her and claimed her lips.

She tasted sweet with little a bit of whiskey...and that same slow burn.

There was no hesitation on her part. She opened for him, melded her body to his and turned him inside out. He wanted more of this crazy girl who made her own rules. Within moments, the slow kiss turned into a fire threatening to burn down every single reason he had for keeping his distance.

Hot and needy, he cupped her neck and feasted on her hungry lips. Her moan mixed with his groan shot him right past the limits he'd tried so hard to maintain.

Her hands crawled under his shirt, scraped across his lower back along the edge of his jeans. This girl had no inhibitions and held nothing back. He coiled her hair in his hand and pushed her to the floor. Need overriding sense, he wanted to bury himself in her.

Get lost in all that was wild about her.

Chapter 7

Oh lord. Thrand was kissing her and she couldn't get enough. Cassie gave into all her pent up hunger, and when he pushed her back against the floor, she hooked a leg around his. No way was she letting him get away again. His body was flush against her, his weight pressing her into the carpet, and she was as close to heaven as she'd ever been. She raked her nails up his back, the muscles there bunching under her touch. His heat surrounded her and she arched her hips feeling just how much he wanted her.

His lips traveled down her neck, making her body shudder. She was beyond thinking. His hands skimmed up her shirt and cupped her breast, sending her right over the edge.

"Thrand." She gasped against his ear.

His body immediately stiffened and he jerked back.

She clutched his shirt when she saw warring emotions flicker across his face. "No. Don't you dare stop."

"But—" He tried to push himself off of her.

"Dammit, Thrand." She tried to pull him down for a hard kiss, but he wouldn't budge.

"You're high." He shook his head and scrambled off her and to his feet.

She launched herself up to stand toe-to-toe with him. "Seriously? Now, it's cause I'm high? For the record, I'm not that high. I know exactly what I'm doing. What will it be next time? I'm tipsy, or I'm wearing purple."

She didn't care that she wasn't making sense. The man was being absurd. He wanted her, but his so-called morals were getting in the way.

He glared at her. "I try to respect you and you throw it in my face?"

She laughed bitterly. "Right. If it was just respect, I could deal with it. But that's not all that's going on here. You and I both know it."

He took a step back and the muscles in his jaw worked. "I'm not talking to you when you're like this."

"Like what? Like when I'm wanting you?" She flung her hands out wide then planted them on her hips. "And you haven't been talking to me at all."

He didn't respond but turned on his heel and went upstairs to his room.

"That's right. Walk away." She was so mad she grabbed a couch pillow and screamed into it.

Five days later, Cassie stood in Lila's apartment. She'd had all she could take and she was pulling out all the stops. He'd gone from barely talking to her, to flat out ignoring her. She'd tried talking, reasoning and flat-out yelling. Her patience was gone. Nothing was getting through his thickheaded skull.

She looked into the full-length mirror and bit her lip, then glanced at a grinning Lila.

"It's perfect." Lila folded her arms over her chest and nodded her head in triumph.

"You think?" Cassie wasn't sure about that. She wore low-rise tight jeans, which were fine, but the top was a black, cropped, skintight, off the shoulder shirt. Her boobs weren't hanging out or anything, but her mid-drift was bare, it was more revealing than what she normally wore.

She was a bit self-conscious, because even though she was tall, she wasn't skinny. Wearing her pajamas around Thrand's house seemed a lot safer than wearing this into town.

"I don't think I have the body for this."

"Don't be silly. You're curvy, and trust me, you're hot."

Thrand was playing a gig tonight at Booseys, and Cassie had the night off. Lila assured her getting gussied up was a fabulous idea and thought Cassie should take advantage of it. Let him see exactly what he was missing. Cassie, on the other hand, had second thoughts. This wasn't how she wanted to go about things, but she'd tried everything else.

"Here." Lila shoved a shot glass in her hand.

"What? Why?"

"Liquid courage."

Cassie sighed, then downed it, letting the burn settle into her toes.

"The boots. You gotta change those. I got some great heeled boots—"

"Oh, no. No heels." Cassie glanced at her worn, punk-style, combat boots. "These are fine."

"All right, but only 'cause you're tall anyway. Now, let's go. I can't wait to see his face." Lila dragged her out the door, giggling the whole way.

The shot was doing its job with Cassie's tension, until they stood at the entrance.

"Well, well, Jailbait. Look at you." Dooley let out a whistle.

"Thanks." There wasn't anything intimidating about him now and she gave him a hug. She pointed at Lila. "Her idea."

Lila's blue eyes twinkled with mischief. "Drastic measures were called for."

Dooley narrowed his eyes and bellowed with laughter, his large frame shaking with the deep sound. "Let me guess. This is for Thrand."

Heat hit her face at the mention of his name.

"That boy ain't gonna know what hit him."

"That's the plan." Lila snickered and pulled her inside.

The air whooshed right out of her when she saw Thrand leaning against the bar with a pretty brunette hovering and giggling at something he'd said. Cassie had no rights on him. No holds or promises or anything at all, but the urge to knock that girl flat on her ass was enticing.

"Oh, this is gonna be good," Lila said.

When the girl laid a hand on Thrand's arm and got closer, Cassie's blood pounded in her ears and she halted in her tracks. She was too enraged to let her tears fall, but two could play his game.

"To hell with him." Cassie turned to Lila. "I think it's obvious where I stand with him and I'm tired of chasing. He can do whoever the fuck he wants."

With that, she sauntered toward bar, gave her hips a little more swing and made sure she turned every male head. She tapped her nails on the bar and grinned at Mick when he walked up.

"Looking good, Jailbait."

"Set 'em up, Mick. I'm celebrating," she said then finally met Thrand's eyes.

He stared at her, his expression blank. The girl who had her arm curled around his never noticed. She was too busy whispering something in his ear.

Mick glanced at Thrand then shook his head and chuckled.

"You got it, baby girl. What are you celebrating?" he asked as he set up two shot glasses and poured the amber liquid.

"Being...free." She lifted a glass in Thrand's direction, downed it, then picked up the other one. "Hey, I can't drink alone. Mick set Lila up, too."

Lila smirked and wiggled her eyebrows as they clinked glasses then downed them at the same time. Cassie didn't look at Thrand again.

To hell with him.

When Thrand saw Cassie, it was all he could do not to gape. Her tanned shoulders were bare, revealing the little indent at her collarbone. How many nights had he spent awake imaging his lips right there? Her laugh was carefree, but when she swung her head he recognized the storm brewing in her eyes. She was on a mission to make his night a living hell, and he had a feeling it had something to do with the girl beside him and the past few weeks of tension.

The only reason he'd even approached the girl was to drive out thoughts of Cassie. But from the moment the girl opened her mouth, he realized it wouldn't work. Her hair was wrong, her eyes the wrong color, and that surgery sweet voice grated on his nerves. He was about to walk away, when Cassie showed up.

His luck sucked ass.

He jerked himself away from the woman and jumped on stage to finishing setting up and ignored Ryan's amused expression.

Over halfway through the set, Thrand thought his head might explode. Cassie had danced with every guy in the place, and it seemed she had finally settled on one—some blond cowboy who wouldn't keep his hands to himself. On the verge of violence, Thrand kept breaking his sticks.

Her hair curled down her back and her hips swayed to the beat of the music. *His beat.* She held a beer high above her head, danced, and completely ignored him. How could she do that when she was dancing to *his* beat?

The song they played wasn't even over when he stood up behind his set, making the rest of the band stop and turn in surprise. He banged his sticks together three times and the noise in the bar quieted a bit.

Cassie turned to look at him, he pointed at her with one stick, then banged them together three more times. Her smile reached him from across the room. She hopped off the cowboys lap and took a few steps toward him through the crowd.

Then he started playing her favorite song. Hard rock all the way. Not suited for Honky Tonk Row at all. He didn't give two shits what he was supposed to be playing. Bedlam was lose and there was only one thing he wanted.

Her attention.

The guys in the band said something to him. He didn't listen. They didn't know the tune. But Cas did. She'd climbed on a chair, rocked it out, and her hair flew wild as she sang at the top of her lungs. The entire bar watched her and she didn't care. Just kept right on doing her thing. Being everything that drew him in.

But the best part? She kept shoving handsy cowboy away.

Ryan caught on and joined in with some guitar riffs that made Cassie squeal with joy. Thrand didn't know why she loved the song so much, but now, she was dancing to his beat and his beat alone.

Adding fuel to his fire.

He'd gotten exactly what he wanted...her focus on him.

People poured into the bar from the streets, filling it to capacity as he played wildly and dumped all his feeling into the song. The crowd jammed with her, Lila included, but he ignored them. Cassie pumped her fist in the air as part of the crowd joined in with the chorus. Her face was flushed, her green eyes flashing bright as they bored into him.

Sweat slid down his spine and the fire she created roared out of control. From the day he found her in Nashville, he knew she was going to be trouble.

She wanted him?

Let's see if she could really handle him.

Cassie had done a good job pretending to ignore Thrand, but there was no way she could overlook the heat from his eyes as they followed her around the bar. She was still pissy about the girl, but when he knocked those sticks together right in the middle of a song, she couldn't contain her excitement.

He played her song. Not caring that all the band members, except for Ryan, were ticked. This was Bedlam. A part of him she hadn't seen in a long time. The crazy, fuck-em-all, guy she knew so well was back.

She was breathing hard when Thrand hit the last note and broke another stick. He stood, sweat sliding down his arms, his black cap on backwards. He hopped off the stage in one smooth move, the intensity on his face had her swallowing hard. He took only a couple of steps then stopped and cocked his head. His lips tugged into a smirk that sent her pulse racing.

He crooked his finger for her to come closer.

She tried not to rush, but she pushed through the crowd toward him, not caring how desperate she might look. She crashed into him, his arms wound tight around her and his lips landed hard on hers. His thrust his tongue into her mouth, demanding, not asking. She matched his ferocity. She'd wanted him for so long, there wasn't any hesitation on her part.

She panted against his lips when he pulled back and said, "You're coming with me."

It wasn't a question. He grabbed her hand and his jacket and hauled her outside to his Harley.

He shrugged on his leather jacket, swung his leg over, and settled in his seat. She fiddled with her leather cuff when he looked at her and raised a brow.

She climbed on. Her thighs gripped his hips, her arms wrapped around his waist, and she tried to even out her breathing. But it was impossible. Not only because she was so close to him but because she had a good idea what was going to happen. At least it better.

He glanced over his shoulder at her and squeezed her hands where they laced together. "Scared?"

"Hell no. I'm ready for this."

Thrand chuckled. "Hold on tight."

He turned on the bike, and the rumble vibrated through her body as they took off. He got them through the heavy traffic quickly and they sped down the road.

His muscles tensed each time he shifted gears and she held on tight. Her hands rested near the hem of his shirt and she shoved them under it. His abs clenched in response and she couldn't stop from trailing her fingertips along the top of his jeans. She was beyond wanting him. It was a need. She sure as hell didn't want him overthinking.

"Fuck, Cassie, if you want us home in one piece, you'd better stop."

She nipped at his ear and his chest rumbled on another curse. Soon, they pulled into his garage and, before the door had even closed, he had helped her off and pounced on her. She fell against the garage wall as his lips slammed on hers.

He took her breath and made it his own, and she whimpered against him. This was him. Unleashed. No holding back. None of their other kisses had been like this. Frenzied and wild, they stumbled up the short steps into his house.

Cassie shoved off his jacket and it fell to the floor. She clung to his neck as he picked her up and set her on the kitchen island then stepped between her legs.

"You've been driving me fucking crazy, woman." His words were hot on her neck and he kissed along her exposed shoulder as he ground into the vee of her legs.

"You better not stop." She wrenched off his shirt, his hat fell to the floor in the process, and she skimmed her hands over his bare chest.

"Too late for that, Cas." He peeled off her top and tossed it.

His hands seared her skin when he cupped her breasts. He pushed her flat while his mouth latched onto a nipple. She gasped and arched toward his lips. Never in her life had she felt like this. Every nerve electrified, her body searched for more. Her legs clenched around his hips. They rocked together with nothing but jeans separating them.

He rolled a nipple between his fingers as his other hand gripped her ass.

"Can I make you come like this?" he whispered against her ear.

She was so close. With his hands finally on her, she didn't have far to go. He ground hard against her and his teeth tugged on her other breast.

"Come for me." His gravelly voice demanded.

"Thrand," she panted. Her nails dug into his shoulders as her body bowed into his.

"I'll take that as a yes." Then he yanked her up. "Hold on."

With her legs locked around his waist, her arms wrapped around his neck, and his hands on her ass, they headed up the stairs. The friction of her breasts against his chest was delicious. She buried her head in the crook of his neck and licked.

His scent, his taste...she couldn't get enough.

He kicked his door, slanted his lips over hers as they stumbled and fell onto his bed.

She didn't care that he was heavy or that the scruff of his beard would leave marks on her skin. She wanted to be marked. She wanted to feel him. All of him. She got his belt undone, but he lifted off her and smirked at her frown. Thrand undid her pants and slowly slid them down her legs.

She watched the way his gaze memorized her skin as her jeans came off. The hunger in his eyes, the way his gaze traveled her body made her squirm in anticipation. Then he yanked her till her legs dangled off the bed.

"I've been dreaming of those legs wrapped around me." He kissed the inside of her knee.

"I can't wait. Please, Thrand." She grabbed his arms, pulled him close enough to shove her hand into his jeans and gripped his cock.

"Fuck." He groaned as he pumped into her hand.

The muscles in his neck stood out. Entranced by the silken feel of him in her hand, she sat up so she could kiss along his stomach.

"Oh, hell no." He stepped back and dropped his pants and boxers.

Six foot one of naked, hard flesh was all hers, but all she could do was stare. Nerves hit. This was really happening. Thrand was really going to make her, his.

"I want them off," he said as he stood over her.

In a trance, she didn't react to his words fast enough. So he did it for her. In mere seconds, he'd pushed her flat and wrenched her panties off. He spread her legs wide and his mouth settled between them. She screamed his name, overwhelmed with the jolt of his tongue on her. She fisted the bedcovers as wave after wave of sensation hit her.

"Mmm." He hummed against her and her hips jerked off the bed in reaction.

She floated on a cloud of wonder. Her body tingled from head to toe so it barely registered that he slid her up the bed and was hovering over her. She heard the crackle of a wrapper as his mouth did wicked things to the crook of her neck.

"My lips right here." He bit at her collarbone. "This spot kept me up at night."

She clutched his shoulders as she tried to keep up with him. But there was no way. She looked up into his eyes as he slid hard into her.

Her body tensed at the intrusion.

He froze and his eyes wide in the dim light. "Cas...what the hell? You're a virgin?"

He filled her. Stretched her, and afraid he would pull back, she arched into him, finishing the job. She whimpered at the sharp pain and shook her head. "Not anymore."

When he tried to move off her, she locked her legs around his waist, forcing him deeper.

"Don't you dare stop," she said near his ear.

"Dammit, girl," he mumbled, took a deep breath and finally moved. Careful. Easy. He kissed the corner of her lips softly, and touched her as though she were delicate. The pain receded and was replaced by an incredible need.

Slow was not what she wanted.

She tried to move more, speed things up, but he kept on with his leisurely pace.

Impatient with his change, she gripped his head and kissed him hard. She tasted herself on his tongue. It spurred her like an aphrodisiac.

"Dammit, Cassie. I don't want to hurt you."

She didn't know the words to make him understand, so she bit his lip and rolled her hips. It hit a spot that made her entire body shake.

Coherent thought crumbled beneath his immediate onslaught. He thrust into her hard and drove away all the black voids of her past. All the pain that had been her life—none of it mattered when Thrand was with her.

In her.

Just him.

Over and over, he filled her. He cradled her leg higher and she cried out. It was like a race toward the peak. It hit and she screamed his name. Sweat rolled off him onto her as he finished with her. Tense and hard, he pulsed in her. She rested her lips on his neck and the spicy aroma of their bodies wrapped around her.

It should have soothed her. It didn't.

She hadn't been saving herself for anyone special necessarily. She just wasn't giving it to anyone in Woodbridge Grove. She always thought sex was just an act. Never thought her emotions would get tangled with it. She didn't believe in happy ever afters. The idea of forever was a crock.

But this wasn't just physical act.

Nothing could have prepared her for this. She squeezed her eyes shut. She'd only thought he owned her before. This...this was more. Way more than she'd ever anticipated.

If she lost him now, it would shatter her.

Chapter 8

Thrand laid in bed, watching the sun peek over the horizon. He looked down at the girl nestled on his chest while her little puffs of air rushed over his skin. Her lips were parted slightly, her lids closed, hiding those expressive green eyes he knew so well. He pushed back strands of her hair and frowned at her peaceful countenance. They had gotten home only a few hours before dawn and after that bit of heaven, he had just lain there. Wide awake. While she slept peacefully.

Guilt ripped him apart.

She sucker-punched him. He couldn't believe Cassie was a virgin...or had been.

Hell yeah, that wild part of him that she'd tore back open was grinning like a fool. The more responsible part of him was horrified. His hand brushed lightly over her shoulder and down her back. Even in her sleep, she arched against him and whispered his name.

He clenched his teeth.

He had just fucked his best friend's little sister. That was something a guy didn't do.

Not only that, he took her virginity.

He slid out of bed without waking her. She barely moved. He stood over her naked form, the sheets tangled around her curves, tempting him to climb back into bed. Into her.

"Ah, Cassie, what have you done to me?" he whispered, before grabbing a pair of worn jeans and headed downstairs.

In his kitchen, he stared at his cup of coffee. He set it down, ran a hand over his face and gripped the edge of the counter. What the hell did he do now? She'd pushed him until he lost control and his hunger for her outweighed everything else. He couldn't undo what he did. As if he didn't own enough shame, now he'd added this.

He felt the brush of hair and lips on his back as hands wrapped around his bare waist.

"Mmm, good morning." She purred against him. The light touch of her lips made him tense.

He turned and pushed her back, but she was having none of it and snuggled right up to him. She felt so good and his body wanted her while his mind screamed obscenities at himself.

"Cassie. We have to talk." He moved her away even though it took every ounce of willpower he owned not to pull her in closer.

She looked up at him with a slight frown. Her hair was a mess and she wore nothing but one of his tee shirts. Heaven help him, she had him spinning, and it took him a minute to gather up his thoughts.

"This was wrong," he said.

Her mouthed gaped and her face turned red. "Wrong? How can you even say that?"

Anger and guilt picked him apart. "You were a fucking virgin. Did you ever think to tell me beforehand?"

She crossed her arms over her chest and cocked her hip, drawing the tee higher.

"I don't know why it mattered. If I'd said anything, this wouldn't have happened." She lifted her chin stubbornly and stared at him.

"You're damn right it wouldn't have happened. Was this some sort of trick? Or payback? Do you have any idea what your brother would think of what I did to you?"

Her face paled before she balled up her fists. "Payback? For what? And who cares what my brother would think. He's dead."

"I care," he yelled. "And for leaving you like I did. I was supposed to protect you. Help you. And I left. I didn't keep my promise to him and now...are you trying to gut me with guilt? You were like a sister—"

"Thrand, I was *never* like a sister to you. Ever. You can preach that to yourself all day, but you know it's a lie. And what do you mean you promised him?"

"I took your virginity," he mumbled under his breath, and looked at her. He realized she was right about the sister thing, but he couldn't stop Cameron's accusing voice in his head. "He made me promise to take care of you if anything happened to him. If Cam were here..."

He shook his head, not finishing. Why couldn't she understand? He'd loved Cameron like a brother. There wasn't anything he wouldn't have done for him, then he died.

And Thrand just screwed his sister.

"You did all you could. Cam knows that—" Her eyes widened, her lips trembled and she backed away from him, putting the island between them. "You think I pursued you...to hurt you...because you left me? Because I knew you would feel guilty about it?"

She laughed but tears slowly slid down her face.

She nailed exactly what he'd been getting at but her utter revulsion made him recognize what an idiot he'd been. He struggled, trying to gain his footing. He never meant to hurt her, but that's exactly what he'd done.

"I may have been mad you left, but I understood it. I wanted out just as badly as you did." She turned on her heel, walked a few steps away, then spun back around. Her red, tear-filled eyes pierced him. "Thank you for taking the most beautiful thing—possibly the only beautiful thing—to ever happen to me and destroying it. What a mind fuck, Thrand."

"Cassie, wait," he said right before she slammed the door to her room. He rubbed his eyes, the pain of it all hitting him. Agonizing words echoed in his head.

He's dead. You just made her cry, you bastard.

Thrand leaned his hands on the cold granite and took a deep breath. How the hell could he fix this? He wasn't sure how long he stood there staring into nothing, but that was the only solution he had come up with. Nothing. He focused on her bedroom door, walked across the room, then paced. He laced his hands at the back of his neck and looked at his feet. He was so confused and torn with guilt.

What could he say? He was at a total loss. Several times he wandered to the door, only to stop. Give her some breathing room. That seemed reasonable. But how much time? Hell, he didn't know. After thirty minutes, he shuffled to her door, dreading the hurt he would see on her face. He still didn't have a clue what he was going to say but knocked anyway.

"Cas, come out. Let's talk about this."

She didn't answer. He was ready to walk in, whether she wanted him to or not, when the doorbell rang. He looked at the time. Who the hell would be here at seven thirty on a Saturday morning? Yanking the front door open, he was surprised to see Ryan, his hair sticking in every direction, a hicky on his neck and his shirt only half buttoned.

"Um, can I come in?" Ryan mumbled on a yawn.

He stepped back to let him. "Something wrong?"

"Uh, Cassie called me," he replied hesitantly.

"What the hell for?" He didn't know what was going on, but he didn't like it.

Just then, Cassie flung open her door so hard it banged on the wall.

"He's giving me a ride. Not that you should care." She stalked across the room, bags in her hand.

"You're leaving?" he asked, shocked. After last night, she was walking out? "You don't want to talk about this?"

She pinned him with icy green eyes, all traces of tears gone. "I think you made things crystal clear. I'm sure as hell not staying here with you."

She turned her back on him and said to Ryan, "Thanks for the ride."

Then she stomped out.

Thrand clenched his hands as Cassie got into Ryan's truck. Thrand turned his glare on his friend.

"I don't know what's going on. She didn't really say. All I know is she asked for a ride to Lila's 'cause Lila wouldn't answer her phone." Ryan dropped his shoulders in defeat. "Cassie said if I didn't come get her, she'd walk."

Thrand shook his head and rushed out to the truck. "Cassie, get your ass back in here so we can talk."

She stared at her hands.

"Come on. Look at me. Talk to me." He heard a sniffle and stopped. "Cas?"

He put his hands on the window frame, trying to peer at her face.

She finally looked up at him, tears streaking down her cheeks. "I might be trailer trash, but I deserve better than being someone's guilt trip."

He dropped his hands and shoved them into his pockets. His eyes clung to hers as Ryan slowly got in the truck and drove away.

The only echoes in his head now were…*You really fucked up this time.*

He made his way into the house, fell on the couch, and stared blankly at the TV. He couldn't believe she left him. He put his elbows on his knees, leaned his head into his hands and memories replayed in his head like broken reel. He thought he'd been happy with his life, but he hadn't been this fired up over anything in a long time.

Not a girl. Not music. Not anything.

When he'd come to Nashville, he'd been lost. Felt totally alone. All he had was a lead, a handful of cash, his truck and a set of sticks. So he'd tried something different. He shoved the

'Bedlam' side of himself in a trunk and did his best to never think of the Daltons or Woodbridge Grove.

He'd succeeded. Mostly. His life was calm but lacked punch.

That crazy girl turned his world on its head. She wasn't simple. She wasn't easy. She was everything he tried to stay away from. She made him lose control.

The doorbell jolted him awake and his neck ached from the uncomfortable position he'd obviously fallen asleep in. He blinked gritty eyes and noticed it was almost noon. He got up, stretched a bit, and ambled to the door. He knew before he even opened it that it wasn't Cassie. She would've just walked in. He opened it, wondering what other surprises were in store for him.

Mick stood there, in full biker gear. Thrand glanced in the drive and spotted the guy's Harley. If he weren't so off-kilter, he would be over there checking it out. But as it was, just being upright took energy.

"Hey, boy," Mick said, then grimaced. "You look like hell."

Thrand nodded, turned and left the door open. He walked to the kitchen to pour out the now cold coffee and started brewing a fresh batch. He heard the door shut and Mick's heavy steps.

He faced Mick as he sat on a stool. "Nice place you got here."

"Thanks. Coffee?" He offered as he waited for Mick to tear into him. There was no doubt he was here to rip him a new one. Mick was always protective of his girls.

"No, thanks. I wanted to come by and tell you how great your gig was last night."

Thrand cocked a brow at him. He didn't believe that for a second and poured himself a cup. He hoped the caffeine would make things seem a little clearer for what Mick was really here to say.

"I had no idea you could play like that." Mick narrowed his gaze. "What's up, man? Something bothering you?"

Thrand laughed sarcastically. "Would you just get on with it? 'Cause I feel like hell, and I have no idea what I'm going to do."

Mick's brows furrowed and his heavy boot tapped his floor. "What are you talking about? Did something happen?"

"You don't know?" Thrand asked, surprised.

"No clue. I just wanted to talk to you about an idea I had. But is there something you need to get off your chest first? Where's Jailbait, by the way? I can only assume it has something to do with that girl."

"Oh hell, Mick. Isn't it always a girl? Especially that one." He took a sip of the coffee, ready for it to start working anytime. "She left me. Packed her stuff and left."

Mick chuckled. "Well, she is a bit of a firecracker."

Thrand sighed and rubbed the top of his head. "I don't usually ask for advice, but I'm really at a loss right now."

"Spit it out, boy."

Thrand sighed and did just that, telling Mick the entire history of him and Cas. He finally paused, swallowed, and blurted out the rest. "She was a virgin."

It was a little refreshing to see that he wasn't the only one blindsided by it.

"Cassie is a virgin?"

"Was."

"Damn. I'm guessing she didn't tell you ahead of time." Mick stroked his goatee in thought. "So you're feeling a shitload of guilt?"

Thrand took another sip of his coffee and wished it were whiskey instead. "You have no idea. I was supposed to protect her."

Mick nodded. "I can't speak for your friend, of course, but did it ever occur to you that maybe he would be happy she was with you? I mean, he trusted you. You know, you don't typically mess with your boys' sister, but there are exceptions. Do you think there might be a chance he's looking down thankful that it was you and not some asshole who would hurt her?"

Thrand rubbed the back of his neck. "No, I hadn't thought of that."

Would Cameron really think that?

"Don't let guilt rip you up. You can't go back and undo it." Mick nodded when Thrand met his gaze. "Now, the real reason I'm here. I want you to start a band."

"A band? You know I don't stick with one band."

"Maybe it just hasn't been the right band. Dude, you packed the house last night with your drum solo. I'm sure you didn't notice, 'cause you played for your girl, but the place was so full, people stood outside listening. Why not start a country band with a little more rock?" Mick grinned from ear to ear, his gold tooth on full display.

"In Nashville? I don't think it would fly." Thrand shook his head, but the idea was intriguing.

"All those people weren't in there because of what the band was playing. It was you. All because of your sound." He slapped the counter and stood. "Think about it. This town could use something different. No one is doing it and you got the chops to pull it off. Listen, I have a couple of guys that might fit the bill. Singer and bass player. Ryan could play guitar. Let me know. I gotta go."

Mick got up and walked to the door, then turned to look at him. "And about your girl? I think you know what to do. Later, man."

For the first time all day, Thrand smiled.

Chapter 9

"**Y**ou're a virgin?" Lila's voice was an ear-piercing screech as she stared at her wide-eyed.

Cassie groaned and put her head in her hands. "Was. I *was* a virgin. Why is everyone so surprised by this?"

"You really gotta ask that? Maybe because you're hot as hell and a tad wild. I'm sorry. I'm just having a real hard time wrapping my head around this. And Thrand didn't know?"

Curled up on Lila's couch, she rested her chin on her knees, letting her hair hide her face. She hated crying in front of people. That she'd done it in front of Thrand pissed her off.

"No, he didn't know. It wouldn't have happened otherwise."

Lila huffed and flopped beside her. "Girl, I'm on your side, but you had to know he would be a bit shocked."

She peered up at her redheaded friend. "Yeah, I could deal with shock. But he accused me of using it to hurt him. To make him feel more guilt. A payback for taking off all those years ago."

Cassie barely held back the tears as she recalled the look of disgust on his face. She deserved him being upset, but not that.

"Whoa, he did what? Seriously, sometimes men are just jackasses."

"Thanks for letting me stay here for a while. I promise I won't be here too long. I just couldn't stay with him." She shook her head. A box would be preferable to living with him. To face him every day knowing what he thought of her. Of that night.

A night she would never forget.

Now she wished she could.

Her phone rang. She saw Thrand's face on the screen. She stifled a sob as she hit ignore. She hadn't had very much comfort growing up, but she didn't stop Lila when she pulled her into a hug as Cassie cried on her shoulder. Tears clogged her throat.

Breathe.

She inhaled deeply, let it out, and looked up at Lila. "Thanks."

"Of course. What are friends for?"

She pulled away, hating the pity she saw in her eyes. "Can I borrow your shower?"

"You're staying here. You can help yourself to whatever, hon."

Cassie nodded and shut herself in the bathroom. Once under the hot spray, she released all the pain she'd been holding in and crumbled into a tight ball in the bathtub. With her fists pressed to mouth, she trembled and screamed into them. She leaned on the tile wall and tilted her head up toward the showerhead. She'd known it would hurt. That if he chose to, he could tear her apart.

She hadn't expected it to slice so deep.

While they'd made love, she was whole. Like all the missing pieces of her were put in place. All the darkness, that had been her life, dissipated.

One night.

A few hours, was all she'd gotten.

Having that peace within her grasp, knowing how it felt, then having it ripped from her so quickly tore bits of her she hadn't even known existed. She choked on how it suffocated and broke her. The spray of water might have washed away her tears, but it did nothing for the ache that had settled like a dead weight in her chest.

Four days later, Cassie grit her teeth as she glared at her phone. How many times did she have to ignore his calls and delete his texts without reading them? She stomped to the bar and shoved the phone at Mick.

"Burn this, or something."

"You know, Jailbait, maybe you should listen to him. Give the poor guy a chance."

Cassie narrowed her eyes. "He talked to you, didn't he? That son-of-a-bitch. How dare he talk to *my* boss."

If she didn't think it would cost her the job, she would throw the mugs against the brick wall.

"Easy there, kid. It was just by chance. I showed up at his house to talk music not hours after you walked. Needless to say, his mind was not on music."

She shoved a hand through her hair, tugged a ponytail holder out of her pocket and pulled it up. "Does everyone know intimate details of my sex life?"

She swiveled on a huff, pasted a smile on her lips to help the customers. But inside, she seethed, especially when she heard Mick's laugh. Men were assholes.

When her shift ended, she wasted very little time getting out and going to a bar the farthest from Boosey's she could find. She was dead tired, but there was no way she would go back to Lila's to lie on the couch and stare at the ceiling, wide awake.

Why wouldn't she answer a single call or text? Thrand sighed and shoved his phone in his pocket. It had been days, and he hadn't, as of yet, been able to catch her at work or at Lila's. She'd done a good job of avoiding and ignoring him.

That night with her had been seared into his brain. Working kept him busy, but he had to sleep sometime, and she was always there. Waiting for him and torturing him in his dreams.

With his emotions doing double time, he poured himself into Mick's idea of a band. Ryan had jumped at the chance and now they were at Boosey's to meet the two guys Mick had mentioned.

Of course, Cassie wasn't here.

Being a weekday, it was slow, so the place was almost dead quiet when two guys walked in. Thrand couldn't help but grin. They had to be his potential new bandmates.

One was really tall, with black spiky hair, and tatted up. The other guy wasn't as big but had long, shaggy hair, and both wore nothing but black. They looked like they belonged on a metal stage. If they had the right sound, they were perfect.

Ryan sat beside him and grinned like an idiot. Thrand waved his hand to get their attention. As the two sat at their table, the big guy shook his hand.

"I'm Ethan Tackett, and this is Zak Hawkins. You must be Thrand?"

Thrand tried not to be shocked by the Georgian accent the guy carried. "Yup. Thrand Medlam, and this is Ryan Fennick, my guitarist. You the singer?"

The guy nodded, leaned back, and crossed his arms over his chest.

Lila stopped at their table with a tray in her hands but took one look at the new guys and froze. He'd never seen her eyes go so wide.

"Are you guys lost?" she asked with no tact at all.

"No. Are you?" Ethan asked.

Thrand laughed. "Lila, this is Ethan and Zak. Part of our potential new band."

"To play what? Thrash metal? Wrong part of the country for that, boys." She huffed and rolled her eyes.

"Well, aren't you in the wrong part of the country? Shouldn't you be at Disneyland with the rest of the pixies?"

Ryan burst out laughing and tugged at one of her braids. "He got you with that one, Lila."

She glared and smacked him with a towel, then batted her eyes at Ethan. "Careful. My pixie dust might be poisonous. Speaking of, what's your poison?"

"Bucket of beer, alright?" Thrand asked the group. Everyone nodded except Zak, who hadn't said anything yet.

Lila brought back a bucket of beer, placed in the middle of the table, and they grabbed a beer. Zak didn't but Thrand didn't think much of it.

"Got any of that pixie dust for me?" Ryan joked and snagged her towel.

"Gimme that." She took it back and hit him on the head with it.

"Owe!"

"Oh hush it, Ryan. The only dust you need is to shrivel your ego. Among other things."

Ethan and Thrand laughed.

"That's just mean." Ryan sulked.

"Pftt. I got customers who probably tip better than you guys." With that, she moved on.

"Tiny, little biddy, isn't she?" Ethan asked.

Thrand snorted. "Mean as hell."

"Got that right." Ryan rubbed his head like the towel hurt him.

After Lila left, Thrand leaned forward and asked, "So what kind of music influenced you guys?"

"A lot." Ethan chuckled and took a sip of his beer. "You know, the usuals, Johnny Cash, Lynerd Skynyrd, Avenged Sevenfold, Merle Haggard. I can sing anything from Strait to Godsmack. Zak writes originals though."

"That's quite a range," Ryan said. "Thrand writes, too. If you ask me, he wastes his time playing other people's shit, when he could be doing his own gig."

"And you waste your time playing with shit quality bands." Thrand looked at Zak. "What kind of stuff you write, man?"

Zak peered through the hair that fell into his face. "Country lyrics. Rock sound."

Thrand grinned. "That's what I'm looking for. If you guys want, we can meet up at my house this evening, test out the feel."

"Sounds good," Ethan said and Zak nodded.

Ryan's phone beeped and he frowned. "Shit, I gotta go. Fill me in later, Thrand."

Before Thrand could ask what that was about, Ryan took off out the door.

Thrand turned his attention to Ethan and Zak. "I think we can work out the rest tonight."

"Sounds good." Ethan gave him a fist-bump. Zak merely nodded his head and they left.

Thrand stayed at Boosey's hoping to catch a glimpse of Cassie, but Mick finally walked over to him. "Dude, she's not working today."

He sighed. "Of course she's not. Has she said anything at all?"

Mick shrugged. "She just gives me her phone and asks me to burn it while she works. She refuses to even talk about you."

"Dammit. If I could just talk to her."

Lila slid next to him. "She's clammed up completely about the whole thing. I know she's never at the house though. I don't know where's she's been."

"She's not staying with you?" A bit of panic set in. It was one thing not being able to talk to her, but at least he thought she was safe with Lila. Now, he didn't even have that. Or even who she was spending time with. Dread slid down his spine.

"Yeah, she is. Kinda. I mean her stuff is at my house, and once in a while, I find her asleep on my couch, but she's gone a lot."

"I gotta find her." He stood and gave Lila enough cash to cover his tab. Then he hit the door, determined to search every hellhole bar in Nashville if he had to.

Thrand pulled up in his drive, late for their first band meeting. He'd had no luck at all finding Cassie and, honestly, with all the people passing through, a person could hide really well in a town like this.

The guys decided to just play some cover stuff to see how they sounded together. Thrand had been shocked by Ethan's voice. How the dude hadn't been signed somewhere baffled him. Not only could he belt the most metal tune Thrand could play, he put a whole new twist on the country stuff.

Before they were done, Ryan got another text. Cussing a blue streak, he was out the door again.

"He got girl problems?" Ethan asked.

"I don't know what the hell he's got." Thrand shook his head and looked at Ethan and Zak. "This was definitely the sound I had in mind. You guys in?"

"Might work," Zak said.

"I think this is worth a shot," Ethan replied and shook Thrand's hand.

Cassie had shut down. She refused to talk to anyone at Booseys, even Lila. She'd thrown up every wall she'd shed when she left Oklahoma. Tell hell with them all. She couldn't sleep. She couldn't eat. She tossed back another shot.

But she could drink.

Thrand saw her as nothing but a mistake and a guilt trip.

It only proved her theory, she didn't want a savior or a hero. When she left home, she'd been so full of hope. So sure she was on the right path. Her luck had to get better because it couldn't get worse. Right?

She'd been so damn wrong.

She was in another bar after getting off work. This one had a mechanical bull and her ass would be on it before the night was over. Her phone rang and she saw Thrand's face. Of course. The man evidently didn't get it. He'd made himself perfectly clear.

He thought she'd used him.

It was a slap to the face. All the years they'd known each other, how could he think she would be like that? She wasn't vindictive. That it even crossed his mind sickened her.

She swallowed her tears, put her phone on mute and smiled sweetly at the bartender. "Another shot. Or three."

It didn't matter.

She knew she was on the path of destruction, but right now she couldn't deal with it. There was a mechanical bull with her name on it and a few cowboys who watched her walk straight for it. Right now, that was all she needed.

A few days later, she stood outside on Broadway, the street packed with people. The Fourth of July fireworks celebration over the Cumberland River was nothing short of amazing. She'd never seen such a display.

Too bad she was totally alone. Which said something about her state of mind. To feel alone yet be surrounded by so many people. Couples kissed, held hands and it did nothing to help the raw ache in her heart.

What she needed was a drink. She pushed her way through the throng, ignored the catcalls, and made her way toward the nearest bar—then stopped dead in her tracks when she spotted him.

Thrand. Her throat closed up.

How she saw him in this crowd was astounding. He looked good. So casual and sexy, all she wanted to do was throw herself into his arms.

Holy hell, how she missed him.

Missed his smile, his touch, the way he moved.

She'd tried to find someone else. Kissed more cowboys than she could keep track of, but she couldn't do it. No matter how drunk she got, she always managed to get away from them. She didn't want them. She wanted him.

He wasn't close, but when he turned his head, as though searching, she ducked and disappeared into another bar. And drowned herself as deep as she could get.

Anything to numb what he'd done to her.

He'd ruined her for anyone else. And it was all her fault.

Cassie had lost track of time. She asked Mick for days only, tried to avoid Thrand at all cost but she barely made it to work at all. Just went through the motions, ignored everyone and just existed. It was the same every day. Wake up, work—if she could drag herself off the couch she slept on, hit the bars then pass out.

After another night she could barely remember, she somehow made it in for her shift. She tied on an apron, ignored Angel's dirty looks, and got busy. She wasn't there two hours when Mick came out of the back and glared at her.

"Cassie," Mick's yelled. "In my office."

Hell. She straightened her shoulders and followed him.

"Sit," he ordered.

She did.

He fell into his cushy office chair, rolled a pen in his hand and said nothing. She shifted. His disappointment as clear as the frown on his face.

"I like you. But I got a business to run. You get me?"

She nodded and rubbed hard on her cuff.

"I'm gonna give you another shot, because I've been where you are. I know what kind of shit is running around in that messed up head of yours."

She grit her teeth. How she hated when people assumed they knew how she felt or what she thought. "You couldn't possibly."

He dropped the pen, laced his hands and leaned forward. "Your dad is a drunk. You ran away to start a new life and run into your past. Shit happens. You either suck it up, or drown in it. It's your choice, and no one can make it for you. Just remember, don't burn all your bridges in the process. You got friends here who will have your back if you let them."

She lifted her chin. "I'm fine."

He chuckled. "Bullheaded little twit, aren't you? I admire that fire but you better control it or it will burn you down. After today, I'm giving you a few days off. Figure it out."

"I don't need days off." She insisted but stubborn pride wouldn't let her beg for her job, no matter how bad she needed it.

"Yeah. You do. Talk to Thrand."

"No." She blanched. "If that's what you require then I quit."

"My advice to you is to screw your head on straight and figure out what you need." Mick stood. "This is it. I think you know where we're at."

She left her shift that day, pissed as hell. Mick was her boss and had every right to fire her. She'd missed days. Even ran out the back in the middle of work when Thrand did show a couple of times. What he didn't have the right to do was lecture her.

Her dad was a drunk. Cam had been a drunk...and she was turning into one. Even though Mick was right, she wasn't ready to face her demons.

She would. Eventually.

But not tonight.

Tonight, she would burn it up until she felt absolutely nothing.

She shoved her hair out of her face, sucked in a breath and walked into what had become her favorite place. The girl bartenders wore a little bit of nothing and danced on the bartop.

"Cassie," the girls yelled as she reached the bar. They reached down, pulled her up, gave her a shot and shoved a beer in her hand.

Time to forget the world. Again.

Chapter 10

It had been two weeks since Thrand had seen Cassie. And even though the band was doing well, the rest of his life was a fucking mess. He was beyond panicky, especially when Lila voiced her concern about most of Cassie's stuff being gone. She was still working at Booseys, but she wouldn't talk to anyone. He'd been all over town, almost every night, looking for her. Except for tonight. He just sat on his couch and nursed a beer.

At a complete loss, with a sick feeling in his gut.

The squeal of tires in front of his house had him getting up, but before he could get to the door, it flew open. Ryan, who had been acting weirder with each passing day, rushed inside.

"I can't do this anymore. I promised her I wouldn't tell you, but dammit, she's gonna end up hurt or dead. Thrand, you gotta do something."

He gaped at his friend, who was out of breath, his eyes glassy.

There was no doubt who he was talking about.

"What haven't you been telling me, man?" Fury hit him. He dropped his beer to the floor and fisted Ryan's wrinkled shirt. "Dude, friend or not, you better start talking."

Ryan didn't fight him, just stood there, his hands limp at his sides. "I don't have time right now. If you want to keep her from doing something really stupid, you gotta come now. I'll talk on the way."

Thrand released him and, within seconds, they were out the door and headed down the road.

"Just listen. She's been a fucking mess since...you know. Anyway, she started hitting every bar on the strip and burning it down. You know what I mean," Ryan said as he drove.

Thrand's jaw clenched so tight, his muscles hurt. Yeah, burning it down. Turning every head then disappearing before things got too out of hand.

"Anyway, she's been calling me. Asking me to get her out."

"What the fuck? And you didn't tell me?" He saw red. Ryan had known how worried he'd been but hadn't said a word.

"Dude. We're just friends. That's it. And she made me promise." Ryan banged the steering wheel. "How the hell did I get in the middle of this?"

"Because you came and picked her up that morning. That's how. Where is she?"

When they pulled up to Lizard Licks, Thrand cursed again. Of course she would be here, the wildest place in town.

"You're coming in with me."

Ryan released a sigh. "Yup. It's gonna take two of us."

It wasn't lost on Thrand that Ryan knew for a fact how hard it would be to get her out of there.

As soon as he walked in, he spotted her, standing on the bar with the other girls, dancing like no one was watching. She wore frayed denim shorts and a soaked white tank top. Her red bra clear for every asshole to see.

Music blared and packed wasn't the word for this place. It was nuts. He shouldered his way to the bar, not caring who he pissed off. By the time he reached her, she was on her knees, her hands braced behind her on the bar. Her shirt was pulled up to bare her stomach, as some dude got ready to take a shot from her belly button.

He shoved the guy and took the shot himself. She laughed and flung herself right into his arms.

"Thrand?" Her shocked face and glazed eyes focused on him.

She'd had no idea whose arms she was throwing herself into. His vision clouded with rage.

"Dammit, Ryan. He promised," she mumbled in a drunken slur and fought him. Truly fought him. Her eyes wild, she swung at him, but her fists glanced off his arms doing nothing but pissing him off more.

"Stop it," Thrand said through clenched teeth. "You're coming home."

Her fight didn't last long. She was too drunk. Getting her out was a bit more complicated. Seemed guys wanted to be her hero and save her. He would have punched every dude in the joint, but that meant he'd have to let Ryan carry her.

Fuck that.

So Ryan did some fast-talking to the morons as Thrand barreled through the throng. They reached the truck and she swayed on her feet. Thrand slid into the backseat with her and held her tightly while she passed out in his arms, her body shivering.

When the truck didn't immediately start, he looked up. Ryan leaned his head on the steering wheel, his shoulders slumping.

"Take us home. She's freezing," Thrand said not bothering to hide his hostility.

"Yeah," Ryan said and had them home in no time.

Thrand moved to get out and bundled up Cassie.

"I'll get her stuff. Be back in a minute," Ryan said through the open window of his truck.

Suddenly, it all made sense. All the weird texts and Ryan's disappearing acts. Lila not knowing where Cas had been staying...she'd been with Ryan.

"You do that."

Ryan looked guilty as hell before he drove off.

Thrand got Cassie up to his room and quickly stripped off her wet clothes. He tried real hard not to stare at her naked body, instead concentrated on getting her dry. Then he slid one of his shirts over her head, giving him a reprieve and depriving him of the view at the same time. She barely woke during the process. How many times had Ryan seen her like this? He tucked her into his bed, and her contented sigh formed a lump in his throat.

He sat in a chair and stared at her face, noticing the dark circles under her eyes, her thinner frame. Was she trying to kill herself? He got up, went to the bathroom, and splashed cold water on his face. He braced his hands on the sink and dropped his head. His imagination was driving him out of his mind. How many guys had she flung those arms around? Had Ryan been one of them? He rocked on his heels, hot fury coursing through his veins.

He wouldn't let her go again.

But he might have lost his best friend. He went back in to check on her and found Ryan sitting on the bed beside her. Her bags of stuff were on the floor. Ryan's hand was on her face.

"Dude, back off," Thrand whispered through clenched teeth so he wouldn't wake her.

Ryan jumped to his feet and quickly headed out the room. Thrand shut the door but didn't latch it so he could hear her if she needed him. He stalked out after Ryan.

"Don't think you can walk out that door without an explanation." Thrand was holding back by a thread. One wrong word and he would snap.

Ryan stopped, just short of the door, and faced him. Weary defeat etched his face. "Just so you know, nothing happened between us. I was only there to get her out of a jam."

"Sorry if I have a hard time believing that considering she's been staying with you and you just had your hand on her."

"Trust me. When she wasn't trying to drink herself into a coma, or having nightmares, she was too busy being in love with you to notice much else."

Thrand jerked. "What?"

"Look, I brought her back to you. Now don't fuck it up." Ryan spat the words and pivoted on his heel.

Thrand grabbed his shoulder and spun him around. "You don't have the right to be angry. I've been trying to find her. You even told me you were looking. For a best friend, you were no friend at all."

Ryan ran a hand through his hair. "I ran into her at a gig. Drunk as hell, hanging all over some dude. I got her out, but she begged me not to tell you. After that, she started calling me when things got out of hand. She didn't want you to know, said it was none of your business. So, I didn't tell you."

"Because she asked you not to?"

"Yeah."

"When did you find her?"

"About four days after she left you."

They glared at each other, and it dawned on Thrand. "You like my girl."

He swung and hit Ryan's face with a thud, almost knocking him to the floor. The urge to finish him was tempting, but all Ryan did was hold his jaw and nod. He didn't fight back.

"I probably deserved that. After you cool off, just remember who brought her back to you." With that, Ryan left.

Thrand wanted to slam the door, but he didn't want to wake her. So he shut it quietly, locked it, and took the stairs two at a time to his room. She hadn't moved. He changed into shorts and slid in beside her. The bed dipped a bit, and she rolled toward him. She was only inches away. He didn't dare touch her, though. Fear held him frozen. When she woke, would she run again?

Her eyes fluttered open, barely, and his name slipped from her lips as she cuddled right up to him. He took a deep breath, and she sighed against him. He wrapped his arms around her and kissed the top of her head.

He hadn't been sleeping well since she'd left, but the peace that had slipped away the moment she'd slammed into his life was back. She was safe. He drifted off, with his hand tangled in her hair.

Thrand woke with Cassie draped across his chest, her little snores telling him she was still asleep. He lifted his head and glanced at the clock. Eleven A.M. He gently tried to untangle himself from her, but her leg was thrown over his, and as he moved, he realized her shirt had ridden up—with nothing beneath. He stalled, half-in, half-out of the bed, staring at the curve of her hip and ass. The blankets pooled around her knees, so he got a great glimpse of leg with the view.

Thoughts halted as the light filtered in through the window and her tanned skin begged to be touched. That snatched him out of his daze. He jerked out of bed and tossed the covers over her. When she didn't budge, he frowned. He touched her face. She was warm, her breaths even, but it worried him that she hadn't woken up.

Several hours later he checked on her. She had moved, but she was still asleep. He sat and gently shook her.

"Cassie. Come on. Buzz, wake up."

No response. Thrand panicked, wondering if she had been taking drugs. He shook her harder. "Cassie. Wake up."

Her eyes blinked open, but they didn't stay open.

"Sleepy." Her words were barely discernible, and she drifted back asleep.

He stepped out of the room, grabbed his phone, and hit Ryan's number. When he picked up, he didn't give Ryan a chance to say anything. "What the fuck has Cassie been taking?"

"What? What the hell you talking about?" Ryan's voice was groggy as though he'd been asleep, too.

"She won't wake up." He'd seen Cam strung out on more than just alcohol and, although Thrand had done some bad shit, drugs were something he stayed away from.

"Dude, chill. If you'd seen how she'd been running herself into the ground…She's probably just tired. She's not taking drugs."

It burned Thrand at both ends knowing Ryan knew more than he did.

"Why the hell was she doing this?" He scrubbed at his short hair in agitation.

"Just talk to her when she wakes up."

"You're not going to tell me anything?" Thrand asked, wishing he could punch him again.

"No. Ask her." Ryan hung up.

"Fuck," Thrand yelled and crushed the phone in his hand. He wanted to throw it but instead, he made another call.

"Booseys. Mick here."

Thrand took a deep breath. "Hey. I found Cassie, but she's not doing too hot. I don't know what her schedule is, but she won't be in today."

"Hang on," Mick said as the loud background noise faded. "Went to my office. Could barely hear you. Cassie's sick?"

"Yeah. Something like that." So Thrand told him the story of how he found her. "She's sleeping like the dead."

Mick grunted. "I'd already cleared her for the next three or four days. I'd told her yesterday to get her act together. Take care of her and get this shit figured out."

"Thanks, Mick."

"Oh and Thrand, don't fuck it up this time." Then he hung up.

If one more person told him not to fuck it up, he would hit something. When his phone rang and saw Lila's name, he ignored it. She would probably tell him the same thing.

He'd been checking on Cassie all day, with nothing to do but pace and think, when he finally heard the shower come on upstairs. It was seven that night.

Finally.

He could breathe. He set about fixing her something to eat.

Chapter 11

Cassie sat up and inhaled sharply when she realized where she was.

Thrand's room.

She put her head in her hands, trying to recall everything that happened last night. Ryan had ratted her out. Damn him. Then she noticed that *all* she wore was one of Thrand's shirts. She frowned when she saw her bags on the floor beside her.

Her hand shook as she stepped into the bathroom and noticed her shorts hung on the towel bar. Oh, yeah. She had been wet.

She took a long, hot shower and used Thrand's soap. His smell brought tears to her eyes, but she refused to think about what she would or wouldn't say to him. Unable to put it off any longer, she reluctantly made her way downstairs.

The smell of eggs and bacon hit her, making her tummy grumble.

She sucked in a breath when she saw him. He wore shorts and a tee, but it was what he made her feel that had her wanting to run out the door. Or tackle him. She wasn't sure which.

"Hey." He put plates of food on the bar and looked at her. "I made you something to eat."

She nodded and sat on the stool. He was so close, she could see the turmoil in his gray eyes.

"Thanks," she said and took a tentative bite. Hyperaware of every move he made, she tensed when he came around and sat beside her, eating with her but not saying anything.

He leaned one arm casually on the bar. His tattooed sleeve emphasized the muscles in his arms. She picked at her food. She was hungry but off-kilter being in his home again. Being near him. Not being able to voice how she felt was suffocating, and after their last words, he'd made it quite clear what he thought about her.

"Come on, Cas. Eat." His voice almost pleaded and she turned to see him watching her, his brows furrowed, his mouth pressed into a frown. She barely kept herself from reaching out to touch those lips.

To hide her trembling hand, she shoved it into her hair. She gazed back at her food, did what he wanted, and drank the orange juice he'd poured for her. She didn't look up until she was done.

"I called Mick. You're schedule is clear for the next few days, so don't worry about it." His back was to her while he set the dishes in the sink. "But you already knew that. From what Mick said you're lucky he hasn't fired you already."

"Why am I here?" She balled up her hands.

He turned and placed his hands on the island. "Because you need to rest, and we need to get shit sorted."

His stare bored into her and his jaw clenched.

Heat filled her face as she got up. "I didn't ask to come here. You—"

"Stop." He held up his hand in warning. "Just tell me one thing. Why couldn't you answer your phone? Or text? Why couldn't you talk to me instead of painting the town red and scaring the hell out of me?"

Her temper rose, until he admitted that she had scared him, which made her pause. But was it some lingering brother-syndrome he harbored? "I honestly didn't think there was anything left to say. And I'm a big girl. I don't need you hovering around."

His stare turned icy. "Really? Is that why you had Ryan saving your ass all the time? Because you could take care of yourself? And I really don't want to get into the fact that you called *him* instead of me."

"I didn't want to be your guilt trip, Thrand. And I sure as hell didn't want you to think it was all some sort of payback." She snapped back.

He shook his head. "I want the real reason you didn't answer me or call me. I don't want any more bullshit."

Her eyes widened as he came around the island, and backed her up to the wall. He placed his hands on either side of her, effectively trapping her. She swallowed, realizing she hadn't seen this side of him. She clenched her fist. How little could she reveal and still pacify him?

She sucked in her lower lip while her heart thumped. She wanted to lie. Tell him to fuck off, that she didn't need him.

"You hurt me. You hurt me like no else ever has. I didn't know how to handle it." That was so much more than she ever intended to say, and the truth was somehow uglier than the lie.

His arms fell to his sides. "Why couldn't you just talk to me? I never meant to hurt you."

"I didn't have the best examples of how to deal with things. It's not like I could talk it out with my old man after he hit me."

She choked and studied the floor. She couldn't look at him. She'd handled this all wrong. She should have answered him. Making love with him had opened her up in ways she didn't understand. So his words, just hours later, ripped her apart. She hadn't known what to do with it all.

He muttered a curse, laced his fingers behind his neck, and looked up. She fidgeted with the leather cuff, as she peeked at him. The way he moved made her insides turn and twitch. She wanted to touch him. Wanted his arms around her.

He dropped his hands and focused on her. His eyes darkened. "Don't look at me like that, Cassie."

She turned away. Looked at anything but him. No need to ask how she was looking at him. Hell, she knew—because it was thrumming through her like a song she couldn't turn off. She'd missed him. Their one night together had been a dream and a horror show all wrapped up in pretty paper.

Before she could move, his hand brushed along her jaw, forcing her to meet his gaze. Anguish reflected back at her. "Please tell me how bad it was. I have to know. Because I know how bad it was with Cam. He hid it from you, but he didn't from me."

Thrand was so close and the rough pads of his fingers made her quake.

"You don't need to know. It's over," she whispered. No one needed to know the hell. She didn't want to relive it. "All it will do is make you feel guilty for leaving. And you don't need any more guilt."

He leaned his forehead against hers. Cupped her face, and she felt the tremors run through him as his jaw worked.

Heat spiraled through her, making her legs wobble. No matter how mad she was at him, there was no way she could deny this. She grabbed fistfuls of his shirt, and stared into his eyes, hoping he could see her. Really see her.

His stormy eyes returned her stare. His breath was hot and fast against her lips. So close, but he held back.

"Dammit, Thrand. Kiss me already." Tears filled her eyes.

His lips landed on hers, tenderly. He kissed each corner of her lips and her jaw. So slow, while his hands held her face firmly in place. His touch was feather light and gentle. Her heart expanded as her breath hitched.

Fast. Hard. Wild—was what she wanted...needed. This slow reverence wasn't something she knew how to handle. She yanked him, bringing his body flush up against hers as she bit at his lips. His response was immediate, his lips slanting hard over hers. Tongue thrusting and demanding entrance. She opened gladly, letting herself get lost in him. No thinking required.

He grabbed both her hips, lifted, and forced her to lock her legs around his waist while he pinned her against the wall. Arching her hips, a thrill shot through her knowing how much he wanted her. Whatever his reservations, he couldn't stop this.

He nuzzled her neck, his lips next to her ear, while he pressed and moved against her. She wanted his skin so badly. Her hand dipped into the neck of his shirt, feeling his shoulders bunch and flex with each grind. He fucked her through her clothes and she panted, on the verge of combustion.

"How many, Cassie?" he growled. "Just give me a number. Because I can't seem to get images out of my head."

She stilled and her eyes flew open, but he was having none of it. His teeth bit and nipped along her neck, sending little shocks of electricity through her. One of his hands had slipped under the hem of her shorts and gripped her bare ass.

"What?" she asked, coherent thought almost impossible.

"Did they make you feel like this?" His finger had slipped easily between her legs, and she gasped, clinging to him so she didn't fall.

A part of her was pissed that he expected answers in such a way, but then he stilled and pulled his head back to stare at her. She tried to move, but he held her still.

She licked her lips and put her heart in his hands.

"I found a line I couldn't cross." Not that she hadn't tried. But no one measured up to him. He was her world whether she liked it or not.

His eyes lit up. "Only me?"

"Oh god. It's always been only you." Her heart splintered, as he demanded it all without giving her anything.

"Thank fuck."

He kissed her hard, one then two fingers moving easily in and out. She broke the kiss and panted his name as he watched her through hooded eyes. Intense. Hard. He ordered her without a word. She shook as she came apart in his arms.

Somehow, he got them upstairs. She wasn't really paying attention. Her world was still spinning out of control. She didn't have a chance to catch her breath, because his hands were pulling her at clothes, his mouth landing on every inch of her skin as it was exposed. She wasn't sure if she helped him strip or if he did it himself. All that mattered was that they were skin to skin.

If she thought their first night was magical, it was nothing compared to this. It was like he knew every secret. Made her body crave more. He rolled to his back, letting her straddle him.

She drank in the sight of him. He was stouter than any alcohol she'd consumed. His eyes were heavy lidded, and his breath heavy, as her fingertips traced his chest and the tattoos that spread down his arm.

"You're so beautiful," he said softly, and his hands slid up her waist to cup her breasts. With his hands on her body but his eyes on her face, her heart skipped a beat. He sat up and captured her mouth with his. So demanding one moment and tender the next, she couldn't keep up. He leaned over, and there was a tearing of paper. She snatched the condom out of his hand and pushed him flat.

She bit her lip, not sure if she knew how to do this, but gently rolled it over his length. He hissed and she ran her hand down him again.

She rose and slammed down on him.

Fuck nice and easy.

"Holy shit, Cas." Thrand grabbed her hips and held her still. She stuck out her bottom lip then tightened her muscles around him. He panted. "Easy."

He tried to make her slow down, but she was having none of it and rocked on him.

Her hair was a tangled mess of honey, her body flushed as she arched her head back when she moaned. He was a goner. She braced her hands on his chest and moved, making her kiss swollen lips part. He couldn't take his eyes off her as she rode him. When she breathed his name, he flipped her and drove in hard.

She annihilated every good intention he had for being nice and gentle. Her legs slid high around his waist, making his drive deeper. She screamed his name, her hands clutching his arms, and it was all over for him. He dropped his head to her chest and breathed her in.

She did something to his brain and all common sense seemed to exit the building. That she had only been with him played like a melody. He had never meant to seem crass when he demanded to know who else she had been with, but she sent him right over the edge of sanity. He didn't even want to think about what he would have done if she had a number.

It didn't matter because her arms were wrapped around him and she was safe.

The rest of the night was spent memorizing everything about her. The dips and hollows, the way her legs slid against his. He reveled in all the ways she said his name. Sometimes begging, sometimes demanding, sometimes challenging. Always surprising him. She wasn't shy.

And with him, there wasn't a line she wouldn't cross.

Those expressive eyes revealed every emotion that flickered like flames in her mind. She gave him everything. Like everything else she did, she did it wide ass open, not holding anything back.

The words she didn't have to say wormed their way in and took a firm hold. He wouldn't name them. He couldn't. Even thought her feelings were crystal clear.

His were a muddled mess.

He blocked all thoughts of Cam and what he might or might not think.

Or at least Thrand tried, too.

But daylight had a way of slapping you in the face.

Chapter 12

Cassie headed downstairs late the next morning. She didn't know what to expect this time. Thrand was full of contradictions. One minute, he seemed totally into her, and the next, she saw shadows of doubt and guilt in his eyes. He couldn't have it both ways. She wouldn't sit quietly while she was someone's guilt trip.

Lost in her own thoughts, she didn't notice until she reached the ground floor, that Thrand wasn't alone. Ryan and two other guys were with him. When a big guy with black hair let out a whistle, she belatedly realized all she wore was Thrand's tee. It covered her well enough, but she shoved at her disheveled hair and met Thrand's eyes with a small smile.

"Hi. Sorry, I didn't know we had company."

Thrand got up, walked to her, and placed a light kiss on her temple. She couldn't read his thoughts, but he turned toward the guys as he stood next to her. "This is our band."

"Ryan told me about it." She glanced at Ryan, but he barely looked at her.

A muscle ticked in Thrand's jaw. "Of course. This is Ethan, our singer, and Zak, our bassist."

Ethan stood, and she couldn't help but stare. He was big. Broad shoulders, big arms and insanely tall. His black hair was in a messy spike and he had almost black eyes. It matched the whole rock vibe he had going on, complete with gauges, tattoos—a lot of tattoos, and a lip ring. When he smiled the hottest dimples she'd ever seen flashed at her. She blinked at the devilish twinkle in his eyes. She might be totally into Thrand, but she wasn't blind. Talk about sex on a stick.

"Hi, darlin'," he said in a very southern Georgian accent that rolled smoothly off a pierced tongue.

Her mouth dropped open. Thrand nudged her and cocked a brow.

She flushed. "Sorry, but have you noticed he sounds nothing like he looks?"

Thrand smirked. "Guys, this is Cassie."

"Didn't know you had a girl, man. Nice to meet you, Cassie," Ethan said.

Zak sat in a chair with a bass in his lap and gave her a slight wave. He had the same vibe as Ethan but was leaner. His shoulder length, brown hair hung in his face, so she couldn't tell much else.

Confused, Cassie looked at Thrand. "I thought you played country?"

He grinned, excitement in his gray eyes. "Yeah, but with a twist."

Cassie snorted and pointed at Ethan. "Well, clearly. How else would you explain that?"

Ethan had sat back down and laughed. "Blunt, isn't she?"

"You have no idea."

"I told you all about the band, Cas. And I told you what we played." Accusation laced Ryan's words.

"You probably did. Sorry. A lot going on." Ryan would know. He was there for most of it, but she wondered at his frown. Thrand tensed and slid a hand to the back of her neck. She glanced back and forth between them as Thrand and Ryan glared at each other.

"What the hell is going on?" They were supposed to be best friends. Instead, they looked like a two dogs with their hackles raised.

It was Ryan's turn to blink, his laugh anything but pleasant. "You gotta be kidding me. You don't know, Cassie? Are you that blind?"

She crossed her arms over her chest, trying to piece everything together.

"Ryan, let it go," Thrand said deceptively quiet.

"Thrand, are you mad at Ryan about me hiding from you? 'Cause if you are, you need to stop right there. That was my fault. You were right. I should have talked to you. Don't be mad at him."

"I forgave him for that already." His eyes were still glued to Ryan, like he was daring him. To do what? Cassie had no idea.

"Fine. I get it. Back the fuck off." Ryan was seated in a chair, and he abruptly got up. "I'll be back later."

He slammed the door on the way out.

Cassie was at a loss and placed hands on her hips. She glanced at Ethan for answers, as if he'd know. "Little girl, if you don't get that they were fighting over you, then you need a reality check."

She crossed her arms over her chest. "Well, that's just stupid."

"Tell you what. Me and Zak are gonna take off, too. Text us when you're ready to play. Later."

With that, they left her alone with a very agitated Thrand, if his clenched fists were any indication.

"Is there something I'm missing?" Cassie asked him.

"You really have no idea, do you? You call him, asking him help you. Watching you drink yourself stupid and no telling what you told him. He said you were having nightmares on top of everything. What did you think was going to happen, Cassie?"

She shook her head. The only thing she'd talked about was Thrand and her feelings for him. But at least the nightmares were gone. "No. He doesn't like me. We're just friends."

"No, sweetheart. He likes you a lot more than that. He only brought you to me when he thought you would end up killing yourself or get hurt."

She backed up a step, feeling the blood drain from her face.

"I wouldn't have killed myself. I might get stupid sometimes, but I would *never* do that." She gripped the leather cuff as tears threatened. "And I don't like him that way. He knows that."

"You're right. He does. Because you're with me."

"Don't go all caveman on me. He knows because I told him I—" She stopped herself and turned away. He certainly didn't need that ammo to use on her.

"What? Told him what?"

She felt him step in close behind her, his hands brushed her hair aside to expose her neck. She inhaled sharply when his lips touched the sensitive spot at her shoulder.

"That you're mine?" he asked and nipped at her skin.

She closed her eyes. Damn the man and the way he made her feel. She whirled around. "Am I? Because last I checked, you were still hung up on the whole your-my-best-friend's-sister thing."

He sighed and rubbed at the scruff on his face, like he did when nervous. "I'm working on it."

"You're working on it? Really?" She clenched her fists and had the urge to knock the hell out of him. "Maybe you need more space to get it figured out."

She stomped to her room, flung open the door...or what used to be her room. The bed was gone, and the room was full of music equipment.

She turned her glare on him. "Where's my bed?"

He smiled and shrugged. "In the garage. We needed the space."

"So where am I supposed to sleep?"

His gaze darkened and he cocked his head, his smirk devastating her senses. "Where do you think?"

"Really?" The thought of sleeping with him every night, well yeah, made her insides turn to jelly, but he didn't need to know that. "How about you sleep on the couch."

She crossed her arms over her chest and tapped her foot.

Thrand stared at the woman. There she stood, wearing his shirt that was barely long enough to cover her ass, exposing those long-ass legs that had been wrapped around his waist last night.

And now she was pissed about sleeping with him? "Is there anything you *won't* argue about?"

Her lips twitched as she tried not to smile and he had a hard time not laughing. She shoved her hair back and pursed her lips. "Not my fault. You're easy to argue with."

He walked over to her and leaned his arm against the doorframe just over her head. "Be honest with me. Do you want to be here? With me?"

He didn't touch her, even though he wanted to. Those big green eyes stared up at him as though searching for something. Normally, he could read her face like a book, but at the moment, she had her walls up. Effectively keeping him out.

She rubbed at her cuff.

"Yes. But," she looked directly into his eyes, "I was telling the truth. I won't be someone's guilt trip. If that's how you feel, the answer is no."

"Can you be patient with me? Give me a chance?" Because he was still torn. He was weighing the advice from Mick, and all his thoughts on what Cam might want, but it drove him crazy when she was away from him. Sure, she had only been here for a few months, but he couldn't remember what his life had been like before her. Except boring. That was all he could remember about it.

She dropped her shoulders and wrapped her arms around her waist. "Working on it. Right."

"Yeah. I never thought about what it would be like to see you again. And I for sure never thought this would happen." Her glare had him rushing his words. "Hold on. Before you tear into me...that doesn't mean I regret it. It means I'm trying to wrap my head around grown-up-stubborn-knock-me-on-my-ass Cassie and the kid I left at home."

Her eyes twinkled, her expression smug. "I knocked you on your ass, huh?"

He shook his head and chuckled. "Out of everything I said, that's what you got out of it?"

"Well, that somehow seemed important."

Her hand played with his shirt, and he hoped that was a good sign. "So, yeah? You'll stay?"

Her face got serious as her hand fisted in his shirt. "I can give you that. But there's a time limit. You either figure it out or you don't."

She didn't have to say what would happen if he didn't figure it out.

He nodded. "That's fair."

She tilted her head, walked her fingers up his shirt, and curled her hand around his neck. She pulled him down to her, but instead of kissing him, she bit at his lower lip.

"I don't share," she whispered.

He grinned against her lips. "Good. Neither do I."

She nipped at him again and, before he could do anything else, slipped away. The hem of her shirt hinted at the slight curve of her bare ass as she walked, hips swaying a little too much, to his kitchen. "I'm hungry."

His mind blanked realizing she'd been standing there in nothing *but* his shirt.

Chapter 13

Cassie sat on the couch, which had been pushed out of the way, so the guys could have room for the band. There still wasn't enough space, but for now, it was all they had.

She sipped on a beer, and kept her camera nearby so she could snap pictures while they played.

It had only been a couple of days since she'd agreed to stay with Thrand. She couldn't help but follow him with her eyes as he set up. They still hadn't gotten everything out but were currently at a truce of sorts. The worst part was keeping her feelings in check until Thrand could pull his head out of his ass. Because every moment spent with him pulled her in deeper than she'd already been. All she could hope for was that he figured it out, and soon. She didn't want to think about what she'd have to do if he didn't.

This was the first time the band practiced an entire set. Their first gig was in a few weeks at Booseys.

"Did you guys ever come up with a name?" she asked.

Ethan looked up and flashed those dimples. "DirtSlap."

She grinned. "Good one."

When the doorbell rang, she jumped up and opened it.

"I brought beer," Lila said as she held up a case, then grabbed her in a hug. "Everything good?"

Cassie nodded. "For now."

"Good." She smiled, pecked her on the cheek, and swept past her. "Boys, I got beer."

"What's she doing here?" Ethan asked, a frown on his face.

Cassie looked between Lila and Ethan as they glared at each other. "She's my best friend. That's what she's doing here."

"Don't worry, Ethan, I won't sprinkle my fairy dust on you."

"And I won't send you back to Neverland."

"Pfft...as if you could," Lila said and gave a little wave of her hand.

"Keep that fairy dust to yourself. I don't need my man-parts shriveled." Ryan covered his crotch, mock disgust on his face.

"Ryan, I'm amazed it hasn't fallen off yet. The number of times I've seen you with hickeys is testament to how easy you are. No telling what sort of cooties you have." Lila inspected him like he might be contagious.

He flashed that killer smile and winked. "Are you jealous?"

"Oh, please! Don't flatter yourself."

Ryan grabbed a beer from her and pulled on one of her braids.

She smacked his arm.

"Owe! Why you always gotta hit me?"

"'Cause you're a pain in the ass."

Ethan laughed. "Ryan, don't let that little imp beat you up. Be a man."

"She's mean. And who knows when she might sprinkle that fairy dust."

Cassie giggled at the exchange, which had Ryan looking at her, all traces of humor gone. He turned to his guitar without another word. She sighed and shoved a hand through her hair. That was one complication she never saw coming.

She took the beer from Lila, pulled out several, and put the rest in the fridge. She moved back into the living room and set them on the table.

"You got water?"

Cassie turned to a voice she didn't recognize and realized it was Zak. It was deep, smooth. It was also the first time she noticed he had extraordinary hazel eyes. His expression was blank, not smiling but not frowning either.

"Sure. Bottled okay?"

He nodded and went back to tuning his bass.

Odd choice of band members Thrand had put together. She was anxious to hear them play. She snagged a couple bottles of water and put them on the table with the beer.

"Who wants water?" Lila asked.

"Zak."

Lila blinked. "He spoke?"

"Does he not usually?" Cassie had only met them a couple of times, so she thought maybe he was just shy.

"Never. They've met at Booseys several times, and I've yet to hear him talk. Or really even see his face for that matter."

"He's probably just shy."

"He's in a band. Doesn't make much sense to me." Lila fell onto the sofa and swung her leg lazily.

"It can happen."

Cassie's attention went to Thrand and Ryan who were deep in conversation. It was hard to believe Ryan had a thing for her. She didn't want to be the reason their friendship ended. She let out a relieved sigh when they smiled and laughed.

She grabbed her camera and zoomed in, catching them in the act. They both looked up when they heard the click. Thrand grinned, and Ryan smirked.

"Liking the camera?" Thrand asked.

"Love it." She snapped another one of just him.

She flopped on the couch with Lila as the guys finished setting up.

Lila slanted her bright blue eyes her way. "This has got to be the oddest bunch of guys for a country band."

"I know. I've only heard them play a little, and Ethan wasn't singing then. I'm sorry, but he doesn't fit this scene at all. Metal maybe. But country? No way."

Ethan looked at them and cocked a black brow. "We can hear you."

"We know," Cassie said.

He shook his head as he adjusted his mic stand. "Thrand, can you control your woman? She's talking shit about me and doesn't care if I hear."

"Not talking shit, Ethan. Just pointing out facts." She flashed him her sweetest smile then winked at Thrand, who merely shook his head.

"Sorry, Ethan. I can only do so much."

Lila snickered. "So do they have a band name yet?"

"DirtSlap."

Lila's brows shot up. "Interesting."

They started by playing the intro to a popular cover song, but what they did to it...and then Ethan began to sing.

Cassie was dumbfounded. The man had the type of voice that slid up your spine. His country twang mixed with an edge she'd never heard before. She knew the tune well, but it sounded completely different with the way Ryan played the guitar. Ethan's unreal voice, and Thrand in the back adding in a lot more drums than the song originally had changed the whole feel of the song.

She glanced at Lila, and noticed she wasn't the only one shocked. She bumped her, and Lila's wide eyes said it all.

"Holy shit. They're good!" Lila said.

When it was over, the girls clapped and whistled. The boys said nothing, and continued on with another song. Cassie didn't know this one. It had to be an original because it was harder and really showcased their talents. Ethan mixed his metal voice with country lyrics and it put a whole new spin on things.

She grabbed her camera and did what she loved. She got down on her knees in front of Ethan so she could get some wild angles of him right when he let go on a long note. She did the same with all of the members. They were unique and she wanted to capture each of their personalities. She got one of Thrand, with his signature hat on backwards, while in the middle of a fast beat with his tongue sticking out at her.

When their set was over, they were all sweating and grinning like fools. Even Zak appeared happy.

Thrand was having the time of his life. This band clicked. Nothing tame about it, but even as he played, he was distracted by Cassie. She danced, her hair flying, hands in the air, shaking those hips in those frayed shorts. She did what she felt without a care. Every once in a while, she looked at him and smiled.

When their set ended, she leaned her head back and laughed. Joy in its purest form. She soaked up whatever life threw at her. How she was so full of life, after the way she had been forced to live, baffled him.

Lila clapped. "That was awesome, guys. Ya'll are going to kill it."

Cassie scooted around the band and equipment and landed in his lap. Sweat ran down his face, but she curled her arms around his neck anyway, and moved in so her breath rushed over his ear.

"You are so fucking hot," she murmured, then used her teeth to tug at his ear.

Blood pumped south as she her tongue danced up the side of his neck. It had him seeing stars, and he barely heard the guys around him laughing.

"Dude, get a room," Ethan said.

He placed his lips against her neck. "Cas, you're driving me nuts. We *are* in a room full of people."

Her answer was to suck on his earlobe, then stare into his eyes, a pout on her lips. "I know. I just had to taste you."

He swallowed hard, then as quick as she was in his lap, she was gone, giving the guys high fives. Even Ryan. It took Thrand a few moments to get his head clear. Her husky words, *I just had to taste you,* echoed in his head and he couldn't wait to get her alone and taste her.

It seemed like forever before everyone started to leave. Only Lila was left, lingering like she was waiting for something, but he had no idea what that might be. He was ready to be rude, and toss her out, when Cassie went into the bathroom.

Lila's crazy blue eyes zeroed in on him.

"I want to talk to you." She grabbed his arm and dragged him outside. He stared down at the little woman, wondering what in the hell she could want to talk about.

"Cassie's a good girl."

His brows shot up, not sure what to say to that. Cassie was a lot of things, but good girl wasn't exactly on the list.

"Don't look at me like that. Just cause she's a lil' bit wild doesn't make her bad." She poked him in the chest as though to emphasize her point.

"I never thought she was."

"I'm telling you this for your own good, and she would hate it if she knew I said anything, but you're so dense sometimes." She pressed her lips in a firm line and paused as though weighing what to say next. "She loves you. You know that, right?"

Brows furrowed, he shuffled his feet. Ryan had said that too, but Thrand hadn't believed it. At least not then.

"Geez, you are dense." She poked him again. "Cassie might seem tough, but you saw what happened the last time you fucked it up. You do it again and I'm gonna tear you a new one."

"Would you people just stay out of it. I'm tired of everyone telling me not to fuck it up. You don't know the whole story. You don't get it—"

"I know enough. Cassie's my friend and so are you. But don't throw away the best thing that's ever happened to you because you're stupid." She glanced in the window then back at him. "I gotta go."

She poked at him one more time, got in her car, and drove off.

He rubbed his chest.

Cassie stepped outside. "Where did Lila go?"

"She left. After lecturing me." He walked past her and back inside. He could hear her bare feet padding after him as she shut the door.

"Oh, hell. She was supposed to stay outta this." She shoved a hand through her hair.

It always looked mussed, but enticingly so, and he always had the urge to touch it.

"I wish they all would," he muttered and popped the top on a beer.

"All?"

"Yeah. Mick, Ryan, Lila. I'm sure more will join in soon." He took a sip as he watched her pace back and forth.

His gaze went to the cuff she never took off. She had modified it a little to fit her. It was worn and shiny in spots where she rubbed it when nervous. Like she was doing now. She was four parts wild, two parts innocent, and he could never figure out which one he was dealing with.

"I don't know what she said, and I don't want to know. But whatever it was, forget it. This is between you and me. We'll either figure it out, or we won't."

Her walls were back up, no emotion at all. He slammed the beer down. He wanted to know if what Lila and Ryan said was true. If what he saw in her eyes was real, he could never get his footing around her. "Dammit, Cas. Don't shut me out."

"What are you talking about? I'm not shutting you out."

"The hell you aren't. You have more emotion in your little pinky than most have in their entire body. So when you say something without emotion, I know you're shutting me out."

Her face paled, then she turned away and shrugged one shoulder. "I don't know what you want from me. I was just stating facts."

He grabbed her and spun her to face him. He gripped her shoulders so she couldn't turn away from him again. "Why do you keep doing this? Keeping me out."

"How can you demand that from me when you do the same thing?" She cocked her head and glared. "Pot and kettle much?"

Stung, he let her go and picked up his beer. "You're right."

"Speaking of walls, how's the 'working on it' thing going?" She tapped an impatient nail on the island.

He closed his eyes. Frankly, he hadn't thought about it. When it did pop into his head, he shoved it away. He didn't want to think about it. She consumed his every thought and kept him spinning. It was easier to get lost in her than think about Cam. He dropped his head because he didn't have an answer.

"You haven't even thought about it. Great." She backed away from him a few steps. "I can't keep doing this."

He swung his head up. "You're not leaving."

"So I'm just supposed to sit here and get all—" She shook her head, ambled to the couch, and plopped on it, giving him her back.

"Get what? Finish what you were going to say."

Her face was in her hands, her knees curled up to her chest, when he strode over to her.

"Oh hell, what does it matter now?" She looked up at him. "To get all wrapped up in you and then you decide you can't handle the guilt or get rid of it. And that's a line for me. I told you that."

Her eyes were pools of green. He couldn't handle her tears, but he didn't know what to do to stop them.

"Did you know, I moved out of Willie's when I was seventeen? I lived at Ruth and Pops in the back room."

He dropped onto the couch, one cushion separating them. He didn't have to ask why. The marks on Cam were proof enough.

"Willie's friends were getting a bit too friendly, and they found my hiding spot at our old fort."

Thrand blanched. "You stayed in there? That wasn't really a shelter."

"No, it wasn't. You guys did a shitty job building it 'cause it was damn cold in there."

He and Cam had built it when they were thirteen. Out in the woods, far enough away that Willie couldn't find it. Thrand leaned an elbow on the back of the couch and rested his head in his hand. He couldn't ask what 'friendly' meant. He didn't want to delve into that. She'd only known him, he had to remind himself of that.

"So you lived in the back room of a shoddy diner." Fury was building. Social services hadn't helped her. No one in that fucking town cared enough to help her.

"It was better than where I'd been. But I never blamed you. Ever." She raised her head to look at him and licked her lips. "I blamed Cameron."

"What? Why?" He stared at her, trying to absorb the fact that she didn't blame him. Never had. Yet she blamed her brother?

"Because we both know it wasn't an accident that killed him."

He felt the blood drain from his face. "You were never supposed to know that."

"I wasn't supposed to know a lot of things. It's funny how you guys thought you could keep me so innocent of everything. It was a sweet but hopeless cause."

He didn't know what to say. She was a smart girl, but they'd done their best to protect her. He thought he was the only one who realized what had really happened to Cam.

"Did you know he was going to kill himself?"

He jerked, the pain twisting him up. "How could you even ask that? Don't you think, if I'd known, I would've stopped him?"

She laid her cheek on her knees, watching him. "You said he made you promise to take care of me if something happened. I just wondered. Not that it matters."

He glanced at her, as he laced his hands together. "You shouldn't blame Cam. You should blame Willie."

"I did. I know why Cam drove off so crazy and drunk. It looked like an accident to everyone but me. And you. But Cam left me alone."

Her voice was so calm, but his gut churned. He leaned forward, hands on his hat and rubbed it back and forth. He'd tried. He'd known Cam was on the edge. Out of control. But he didn't realize he would actually follow through on his occasional mention of suicide. How many nights had he lain awake wondering if there was something he could have done to change the outcome?

"I tried. I was so fucked up. I didn't know. I tried to help you. I failed at it all. Failed my parents..." It just went on and on. "I was never good enough for them. Didn't fit in with their little ideals of perfection. Pissed as hell I was friends with the Daltons. Fucking failure."

He grit his teeth and squeezed his eyes shut. The door he kept firmly locked burst open. It had taken him a while to shove all that shit in there and lock it down. The guilt. The pain.

It flooded him.

Smothered him.

It was a vise squeezing his chest, making it hard to breathe.

The image of Cam lying lifeless in that casket, while Cassie cried on his shoulder—Thrand took the blame for it. If he'd been in the truck with him, he wouldn't have done it. Cam wouldn't let him go with him that night. He'd gone alone.

Then he'd driven off that goddamn bridge.

"I should've been able to save him. Save you."

Chapter 14

Cassie sat numbly as Thrand shot to his feet. She got a glimpse of his face and her breath caught. She jumped up and grabbed his shaking hands. "Thrand, look at me."

He tried to push her away but she clung harder.

"No. Don't you do this. You're not the reason he died. You didn't fail me, and fuck your parents."

He wouldn't say anything. His entire body trembled, the pain etched in his face pierced her heart. His eyes were frantic, as though searching for some way to escape.

"Dammit. Look at me." Scared out of her wits, she shoved him back onto the couch. Before he could get up, she straddled him. She placed her hands on either side of his face, forcing him to focus on her. "There's nothing you could've done. You know how stubborn he was. Once he got a thought in his head, no one could change it."

His chest rose and fell with his rapid breathing and his panicked gaze bored into hers. "I should've known. I failed. If I'd been in the truck with him—"

"No." She shook her head. "It wouldn't have stopped him. If not that time, another time. You did not fail."

He was so crazed for a moment, he resembled Cam when he left that night. She shook her head as tears flowed unchecked down her face. "Even if you had known, it wouldn't have made a difference. I only asked if you knew. I don't blame you for it. You didn't fail me or anyone else."

How she wished she could take back those words. He'd hid it so well. She thought he was past all this. His life seemed fine. He was easygoing, not the high-strung young man she'd known. How wrong she'd been.

He gripped her face and his thumbs brushed away her tears. "Don't cry."

She choked, and more tears flowed. Here he was, dealing with all that baggage, yet he was concerned with her tears.

"Promise me you won't do that. Ever. For any reason," she begged. Her tears slowly turned into sobs. "Please."

"I promise. I won't." His breathing slowed and the crazy left his eyes as he focused on her.

She clutched his shoulders, fear forcing her to make sure. "Promise me. Never. You can't do that to me."

"I won't. I promise." His words were nothing but a strangled whisper.

A scream built inside. Her mind twisted the image of Cam's body, lying in the casket, replacing it with Thrand's. The agony congealed into a mass of ugly cries.

Strong arms wrapped around her as she collapsed on his chest. She clung to his shirt while he caressed her head. She hadn't really cried over Cam, not since the day of the funeral. She'd dealt with her brother's death, but wasn't strong enough to deal with losing Thrand. If he left her, it would kill her.

"Cas, it's okay. I'm not going anywhere."

She clung tighter. She thought, if she could just hold onto his shirt, he wouldn't disappear. Like everyone else in her life.

She lifted her face to look at him. She was a mess, but what if she never got the chance to tell him?

What if something happened?

What if she missed her chance?

Panic seized her.

What if he rejected her? But her fear of him never knowing was greater. She swallowed hard and took a deep breath.

"I love you," she stammered. Heart in her throat, she begged him with her eyes not to walk away. Her hands fisted tighter in his shirt, hanging on for dear life. "I always have."

He appeared shocked and his hands stilled. She thought her heart might thump out of her chest if he didn't say something. Anything was better than silence. She could see he was thinking hard, but she would scream if he didn't say something.

She expected surprise, so when his face relaxed, she released a breath.

"Do you think Cam would be glad?"

Her mouth dropped open. She thought anything was better than silence. How dare he bring this up again? Anger boiled the tears away. "You can't be serious?"

"About this." He leaned forward and kissed her softly, his fingers sliding under her hair to her nape.

She closed her eyes, blocked what he did to her senses, and concentrated on what he said. "I don't care what Cam thinks, and I need you to not care about it, too."

"I can't not care. But I think he might be happy that his best friend, and his little sister are together." He laid a kiss near her ear.

Her body hummed, she wanted so badly to sink into him, but she couldn't figure out what he was saying. She backed away from him but his arms kept her from going too far.

"You have to want me for me. Not some idea that you're taking care of his sister." She was seething. Not comprehending how he thought that would be enough.

He tilted his head, and looked at her askance. "I want you. That crazy-ass girl who knocked me flat on my ass. The one who has my head spinning until I don't know which way is up. The only girl who has me wondering what the hell she'll do next. The one who lit that fire I'd killed when I got out of Oklahoma. I promise you that has nothing to do with Cam."

Rendered speechless, she could only stare as his lips slowly curled up into a wicked grin that made her mouth dry.

"Yeah, crazy girl. That's you. It's an added bonus that maybe, just maybe, he would like that I'm in love with his little sister."

Her heart thundered in her chest. Did he really mean it? Was he saying it just to make her feel better? Did he feel sorry for her? She had the insane urge to run out the door.

His calloused hands held her face, his gray eyes filled with emotion.

"Quit overthinking. That's my job." He leaned forward and rested his forehead on hers. "Belong to me. So I can quit driving myself nuts. Let me love you, Cas."

She was afraid to believe he wanted her. But the intense look in his eyes told her this was the real deal. For once, she didn't have to hide her feelings. Her shaking hands traced his face. Lips. They parted and he nipped her thumb. "You realize if you ever try to leave me, I *will* hunt you down, right?"

He grinned. "Is that right?"

"Mhmm. I'd be that psycho, trailer trash, white girl stalking you until you came to your senses."

"I can see that. But that's okay. If I'm ever that stupid, I give you permission to take out all your insane on me."

"Promise?" She curled her arms around his neck, pressing her body flush against his. She slid her hand up the back of his neck and nudged his hat off and onto the floor.

"You got it, Buzz." He pushed his hands into her hair, and bit lightly at her lips. He kissed along her jaw, sending jolts through her body. She felt his lips twitch against her skin. "Crazybuzz."

"Not Buzzkill?" She sank lower, gripped his hips with hers, and tilted her head to the side, giving him total access to her neck.

"Hell no. You've had me buzzing like a bee from the moment you puked on my boots." He chuckled and she laughed with him—until his palms skimmed under the hem of her shirt. She gasped, loving the feel of his rough hands on her skin.

He caught her lips with his. Gentle was his game, but she wanted that oblivion only he could make happen. Impatient, her tongue met his wildly. He pulled back.

"No. We're doing this my way. And I'm going to make love to my girl."

She frowned. He shook his head, moved her off of him, and waved for her to go upstairs. Her nerves were stretched taut as she walked in front of him. This wasn't how they did this. Normally, it was like adding fuel to fire, instant combustion.

They'd barely reached the top floor when his hands landed on her hips, and jerked her against him. He snagged her shirt, whipped it over her head, and his eager fingers flicked off her bra. She smiled. This didn't seem slow at all. She wriggled her ass against his straining jeans, gripped the back of his neck and arched. She peered up at him and licked her lips.

"You play dirty." His words hot and heavy in her ear. He pulled on a nipple, shoved his other hand into the front of her shorts and slid a finger into her. She gasped, her knees threatening to buckle beneath her.

"Stay right there," Thrand ordered.

Her nails dug into his neck as he slid his finger back and forth. His other hand did wicked things to her breasts, as his teeth tugged at her ear. It was slow torture. His movements unhurried.

"Just like whiskey." He breathed the words into her ear. "You leave that same burn. Except you burn only for me."

He turned her head, kissed her, and his tongue mimicked the slow slide of his fingers. She moaned and tried to move her hips faster, but he tightened his hold on her face. All she could do was stand there and take it.

"Please, Thrand." It was painful being so close to release, yet not there. He turned her, shoved her shorts down, as she pulled off his shirt and unbuttoned his pants.

"Dammit, Cassie. I can't be slow. I want you." He pushed her onto the bed. "Now."

He growled as he fell on top of her. His weight settled between her legs, and in one move, slid in.

"Yes!" There was nothing like him over her. In her. She was whole. Complete.

He shoved a pillow under her hips so every drive hit the nerve that made her body quake. He grabbed her hands and held them over her head as he ground to a halt, buried deep within her. He filled her. Stretched her. But held still.

His breath was harsh and fast as he searched her face. With her wrists firmly pinned in one hand, his other wandered down her neck and over her breast. She tried to move, but she was once again unable to move.

"What are you doing to me?" She panted as his fingers rolled a nipple back and forth.

"I wanted slow. You won't let me have it. So I'm taking it."

With his eyes fastened to hers, he stroked in and out. She strained against him and closed her eyes.

He stilled.

"I want to show you how much I love you."

"By torturing me?" Sweat beaded on her skin.

"Keep your eyes on mine and I won't stop." He dropped a kiss to her nose and his stubble scraped along her cheek.

He moved again, but she obediently kept her eyes open. Love and lust swirled in those gray depths as he drove in measured strokes. It rocked her. Thrilled her. She whimpered, as he did exactly what he set out to do.

Made love to her. With this body, with his eyes.

"I love the little sounds you make. And the way your eyes light up every time you look at me."

He drove in harder, and she cried out louder.

"Mmm, and that one." He licked at her neck. "And the way you taste. And the way you want to taste me."

He pushed her deeper into the mattress. She was lost in his words. Her world narrowed to him. Everything he'd ever meant to her. He stripped her. Left her soul exposed, and bare for him to see. She'd been his forever, but now he owned her completely.

He dropped his head and kissed her. Hot, demanding. She opened to him. Their tongues tangling together as he thrust faster.

"I fucking love you." He groaned as he released her hands and gripped her hips, driving in deep.

She hung on as he kept up a pace that brought tears to her eyes. Spasm after spasm hit her in waves that seemed never-ending. She screamed his name, as he pulsed within her. She drifted on a daze of wonder, as he lay heavy on her. He ripped the pillow out from under her and they fell flat on the bed. His damp head rested on her breasts, and her hands slid around his wide shoulders.

"I fucking love you, too." She licked parched lips, placed a kiss on his neck, and giggled.

He lifted his head. "What are you laughing at?"

"You still have your jeans on."

She couldn't see them but had felt them with her legs.

"Damn, I didn't notice." He kicked off his jeans, and pulled her in close.

Chapter 15

A few weeks later...

Thrand's life was anything but boring. He and Cassie were settled. Sorted through their issues, at least the big ones, and he was over his doubts about whether Cam would approve or not. He would never know for sure, but he knew he loved that girl. That was enough, and there wasn't any way he would let her go at this point. Although settled might not be the right word to describe their relationship.

Cassie argued about everything.

She pushed his hot buttons like no one else, and he never knew what crazy stunt she would pull next.

He laced his hands with hers as they walked toward Booseys, and he stared at her upturned face. Those green eyes danced with excitement. Her honeyed hair loose and wild framed her face as she smiled at him.

He wouldn't change a damn thing about her.

Dooley sat in his usual place at the entrance and pulled down his dark shades. "Thrand, you're one lucky bastard."

Thrand smirked and gave him a fist bump. "Don't I know it."

"Good thing you got over your stupid. 'Cause if I was few years younger, you would've never gotten the chance." Dooley waggled his bushy brows.

"We were both stupid. And you know, if Thrand wasn't around, you might have your hands full." Cassie's eyes twinkled with mischief as she kissed Dooley's cheek. "You're sweetie, Dooley."

"I've been called a lot of things, darlin', but sweet hasn't been one of them," Dooley chuckled. "Don't tease an ole geezer like me. I'm good with watching Thrand try and rein you in."

Her head fell back on a throaty laugh. Her bare neck tempted Thrand because he knew exactly how fast he could make her pulse throb right there.

"Not happening," Cassie said, and those wicked eyes landed on him. "He knows better then to even try."

Thrand winked at her. "Why would I want to?"

She curled her hand around his arm, and leaned up to kiss him. "Smart man."

He returned her light kiss, and shook his head when her teeth tugged at his lip before he pulled away.

"Like I said, lucky bastard," Dooley muttered then pointed at a flyer on the window. "You ready for your set?

DirtSlap was printed in big jagged font, with a picture of their band in the background.

Cassie had taken all the pictures, and designed the whole thing. It looked amazing. She'd even signed up for photography and graphic art classes. He was damn proud of her.

"I'm stoked, man. And we're as ready as we'll ever be. Just hope we don't empty the place with our sound."

"Gotta say, I'm looking forward to hearing this." Dooley popped his large knuckles and flexed his hand. "Mick said you guys got it."

"This was Mick's idea. I just hope we do him proud."

Cassie grinned at the flyer. She was thrilled with how it turned out. She'd taken a ton of pictures of the guys, settling on one had been hard. But this one, with Ethan front and center, was awesome. He was the perfect lead singer.

She glanced at Thrand as he talked to Dooley. She hadn't paid much attention to the last of bit their conversation. Hearing the gravelly tone of Thrand's voice and feeling his hand cupping the back of her neck was enough.

He was hers. She felt it every time he touched her.

She leaned against Thrand, and said to Dooley, "You'll love them. Trust me."

She went inside, Thrand following closely behind.

Her skin prickled. It gave her a little thrill knowing he couldn't keep his eyes off her for long.

"Hey, Jailbait." Mick put a beer in front of her.

"Thanks." She placed her camera bag on the bar, and turned in time for Thrand to nuzzle her ear, his hands on her hips.

"Looking good in those jeans, Buzz. You think you can behave yourself?" he whispered and gave her a little squeeze.

She slid her tongue along his lips. "What do you think?"

"I think you don't know how. But try, 'kay?"

"All right, you two. Break it up." Lila slid beside her, and wagged her finger at Thrand.

He grinned, and smacked Cassie's ass, making her squeak. "Keep her out of trouble, Lila."

He walked off to greet the rest of the band as they carried in their equipment.

Lila sighed, and draped an arm over Cassie's shoulders as they watched him stride away. "Girl, I'm sorry, but that's one fine man. Such a nice ass."

Cassie swiveled her head and eyed her friend. "I didn't think you saw him like that."

"Are you kidding?"

"I thought you were...uh..." She didn't know how to say it without sounding rude.

"Gay? You thought I was gay?" Lila screeched.

Mick's laugh boomed behind her, and Lila looked at her like she'd grown horns. "Well, I never see you with any guys and—"

"Oh girl, you kill me. Believe me, I'm into the guys. Just picky."

"Nope. She's just mean, and guys have no idea how to handle her," Mick said.

Lila stuck her tongue out at him, then turned so they faced the guys setting up. "Don't listen to him. See Ethan, now that boy is hot as hell. And no one, not even you, can say you haven't noticed. And Thrand, of course. We agree about that one."

Lila whispered as she leaned in close, even though Lila didn't really whisper anything. "Ryan, he's almost the boy next door, until you see his grin. Cute as fuck, but such a pain in the ass. But Zak," she paused, "that's the one who will steal your heart if you're not careful. Such quiet intensity. You can never figure out what's going on in his head, yet you're dying to know."

Cassie blinked as her friend scrutinized Zak. Did Lila have a thing for him? "You're right. And he has incredible eyes."

"You noticed that, too? Damn shame we don't get to see them often. All that hair in his face." Lila shook her head, then smiled. "Oh, forgot to tell you. We got a new girl."

She pointed at the woman who just walked in.

She had long, dark hair, shorts, and cowboy boots that went perfectly with the Booseys shirt she wore.

Lila waved, drawing her to them. "Shelby, this is Cassie."

Cassie took her hand and shook it. "Hey, welcome to the club."

"Thanks. Nice to meet you," Shelby said with her eyes glued to the stage.

Cassie grinned when Shelby's mouth dropped slightly. "Before you ask, yeah, they're country but with a little dirt."

Shelby turned back to them briefly, before sneaking another peek at the guys. "He's huge and definitely not country."

"That's Ethan. Wait 'till you hear him sing," Lila said on a sigh. "He sounds better than he looks, if you can believe it."

Shelby's brown eyes widened. "I'll have to take your word for it."

"The guy on drums is Thrand. Zak is the bassist and Ryan is on guitar," Cassie said. "DirtSlap. This is their first official gig."

"You know a lot about them." Shelby tied an apron around her waist.

Lila sniggered. "She would. She's banging the drummer."

Heat hit Cassie's cheeks and she elbowed Lila. "Geez, you make me sound like some groupie."

"Well, it's the truth." Lila patted her cheeks. "Don't worry, Jailbait. We know you love him."

She left her with Shelby.

"Jailbait?"

"I'm legal. Long story. Believe me, it's better than what I used to be called." Cassie waved her hand and took a sip of her beer. "This your first night?"

"Yup. Do you work here?"

"I do. But tonight I'm taking pictures." She tapped her camera bag for emphasis. "Hope you're ready for a busy night. Once they start playing, I have a feeling this place is gonna be hopping."

"I've waitressed before."

The girl was pretty, but sadness lingered on her face. She also appeared a tad nervous the way she crossed her arms around her waist, her too-wide eyes drifting over the small crowd before they settled on the stage again. Cassie understood the feeling and pulled out her camera.

Ethan stood still, mic in his hand. He had mirrored shades on, so she couldn't tell what he was looking at, but it would make a great picture.

"Lila is the best, so if you have trouble, let her know. Or Mick."

"Thanks. I will."

Cassie meandered through the tables, stopped, and aimed her camera at Ethan, who hadn't moved, and snapped a pic. His shirt didn't have sleeves so it showed off all his tatts and muscles. The angle made him look even taller than he was. The band had worked hard to get to this point, and she couldn't wait to see the show on stage. Her heart raced in anticipation.

Her eyes met Thrand's, and she smiled as one corner of his lips lifted slightly. It still didn't seem real that he belonged to her. She sucked in a breath as he hopped off the stage next to her. His shoulders shifted with his body. It sent a thrill of awareness through her. Would she ever get tired of watching him? She didn't think so. Some might misjudge him as smug, the way he moved, so sure of himself. He'd always had that, even when they were kids. Between Thrand's cockiness and Cam's recklessness, they had been quite the pair.

The pain of missing Cam slapped her. It took her by surprise, came out of nowhere, and hit her like a jolt. As much as she liked Ryan, Cam should be the one playing on guitar right now. Her happiness dimmed with the reminder of all he had missed by driving off that bridge.

Thrand touched her face, concern creasing his brow. "You all right, Cas?"

She nodded. Tears threatened, but didn't fall. "Cam would be so proud of you."

He cocked his head, making her heart flutter. "You think so?"

"I know he would." She tightened a hand his shirt. "I wish he was here."

"So do I." He cupped the back of her neck, and drifted closer.

She gripped her cuff.

Cam's cuff.

Thrand tilted her head up. "We can handle it. We're making better memories. And he will always be a part of us."

She met his intense gray eyes. Her world stood right there. She would go wherever he went. Moments were just that. A slip of time, and that's all it took for everything to be taken away.

"I love you," he murmured. His fingers slid along her jaw, and he kissed her gently.

She rested her head on his shoulder and breathed. His words seeped into her, and she soaked them in like a sponge. No one had said that to her. Not even Cam.

She'd never believed in the happy-ever-after, but she believed in him. In them. Their feelings were rock solid.

She wouldn't waste what life had to offer.

She plastered her body against his and kissed him hard and deep. She drowned in his taste, and the arms that held her. She smiled against his lips and said, "It's time to rock this house."

He grinned. "That's my girl."

Available May 2015

WRECK

DirtSlap Series
By
Ashlynn Pearce

Chapter 1

The white house with the chipped paint and rickety porch screamed at Shelby Renner. Weeds grew tall in the yard and the concrete steps were cracked and crumbled. Her heart ached. Tears crowded her throat and spilled down her cheeks. The last time she'd seen the house, the paint was crisp, the yard well-tended. She should have come sooner.

She'd called Gran often but had no idea she had been in such poor health. Not until she got the call telling her she had died. Gran loved this home and wouldn't have let it fall into such disrepair if she'd had a choice. Gran lied to her. She had been sick a long time.

She paced the driveway and her hands shook. If the outside looked this bad, what would she find on the inside?

She took a deep fortifying breath and walked down the cobbled path. Vines choked the rose bushes and the pink blooms were lost in the mess. Gran had taken such pride in her flowers and it saddened her to see them in such disarray. The porch ran along the entire front of the modest house. She could almost see Gran, sitting in the old wooden rocker, a smile on her face.

She sucked in her lower lip. *You can do this.* On leaden feet, she forced herself up the steps. She opened the wooden screen door, unlocked the main one and went inside.

She froze in the doorway. Boxes were stacked floor to ceiling and a thick coat of dust covered everything. She covered her mouth in horror. Gran was a neat freak. This...this was heart-wrenching.

Shelby's gaze landed on the little white doily on the recliner and she fell back against the door. Gran would rest her head right there while napping.

Shelby sank to the floor and leaned against the closed door. Sobs tore her heart as she curled into a ball. She let the pain wash through her and squeezed her eyes shut.

Curse her mother and step-father for not letting her visit more.

Curse them for taking her away from here to begin with.

After giving herself a few moments, she rose to her feet and dropped her purse and keys on the side table near the door. Gran willed everything to her. The house, all its contents and the meager account she'd lived on. Much to the ire of her mother, Camellia, Shelby insisted she needed no help from her to sort through things.

Camellia could care less about anything that belonged to Gran, even though she was her mother. After years of living under Camellia and her husband, John's, thumb, she was more than ready for a break. At twenty-two, she could make her own decisions. School could wait.

Too bad she hadn't had the guts to stand up to them sooner.

She walked through the house, amazed how nothing had changed. Except for the boxes, time stood still. The same lace curtains were on the windows, the same little towels hung in the kitchen. All faded and dusty but still the same. The little knick-knacks and Gran's porcelain collection of tiny cats sat in the hutch, just like they always had.

She swallowed her tears. Falling apart was not going to get her through this. She wandered around the home she'd lived in until she was ten. So many happy memories. She went upstairs and stepped into her bedroom. Her assortment of unicorns still littered the room, as though waiting for her to come back.

Ugly cries hit hard as she sat on her bed and bawled.

A week later found her in a bigger mess than when she started. No small feat to tackle all that was crammed into each nook and cranny. One thing it did do was put perspective on her overbearing parents. She didn't want to return to Houston, where her every move was scrutinized. So, even though she hated confrontations, especially ones involving her parents, she called her mom.

"Hi, mom."

"Darling. Do tell me you're on your way home."

"About that—"

"Yes, I'm talking to Shelby. She's coming home."

Shelby closed her eyes in annoyance. She knew her mother wasn't going to listen to her, but she'd not even given her a chance to talk

"No, mom. I'm not."

"What?" Camellia's screech had her pulling the phone away from her ear. "Yes you are. You're getting married remember?"

Shelby slumped in a chair and rubbed her head. "I need to go through Gran's stuff. It's important."

"What's important is your wedding," Camellia said, her voice cutting. "I didn't go through all the trouble of finding you a fiancé just so you'd be off wallowing in that god awful city. You will come home Shelby Renner."

"How about this. You plan it. You'll do a much better job than me. I'll be there when I need to be." Even if Shelby were there, she wouldn't get a say in anything anyway. Maybe this way she could get her mother off her back. Because telling her how important Gran's home was to her wouldn't make a difference.

"Oh, that's brilliant, darling. You are so right. You have no taste for these sort of things. It will be spectacular!"

"Sure. I'll call again soon. Bye."

Shelby hung up and tears stung her eyes. What a farce.

How could her mother push her buttons from hundreds of miles away? It showed just how pathetic she was. She rubbed at the pain between her eyes.

Shelby eyed a porcelain calico cat. "Sorry about that, Ginger. Hopefully, I won't have to talk to her again anytime soon."

She reached into the hutch and picked up the figurine. Its tiny eyes stared up at her, its little paw raised as though asking for something. This one had been Gran's favorite and she had heard many one-sided conversations between them. Tears blurred her vision.

"I miss her too," she said quietly and put it back in the hutch. "If I'm staying here, I need a job."

She sighed and shook her head. No way in blazes was she asking her mom for money.

Shelby's feet hurt and securing a job in downtown Nashville looked grim. Every place she went took one look at her, heard her Texas accent and automatically assumed she was here to sing. Telling them she wanted a waitressing job just got her laughed at. They would sweep her from head to toe and say, "Sure, honey."

By the time she reached a place called Booseys, she squared her shoulders and marched to the bar. Tall and lean with a scraggly goatee, the bartender looked down at her. She paused. Although she had gotten over the initial shock of the type of people who ran bars, this guy looked more unsavory than the rest.

"What you drinking, doll?"

"Nothing. I want a job—"

"Not hiring," he interrupted before turning his back on her.

Heat hit her cheeks at the condescending tone.

"I don't want to sing. I can't sing a lick even if I wanted to." Her words came out in a rush but he kept walking away. "I'm only here because my grandmother died. I need a job. I sure as heck don't want to ask my mother for money."

She clamped a hand over her mouth. Her emotions got the best of her, again. Stuff she should keep to herself always tumbled out. Sick with embarrassment, she spun on her heel to leave as quickly as possible. She didn't want to hear his laugh, or worse, see his pity.

"Doll, hold up."

She stopped just short of the exit.

"Turns out, we have a gig tomorrow night. A new band, I think it's gonna be hopping. Can you handle a crowd?"

She turned around hesitantly and took two steps to peer into his face. Was he serious? He had flung a towel over his shoulder and eyed her speculatively. No humor, no pity, just a question.

"I worked at a restaurant near a college campus in Houston. It got busy."

He paused for a moment, then nodded. "We can try it tomorrow night, see how it goes. I'm Mick, owner of the place."

She offered a tentative smile and shook his hand. "Shelby."

"Lila," Mick shouted and a tiny little red head skipped over to the counter. He motioned to Shelby. "She's your new coworker, at least for tomorrow night."

"Terrific!" Lila turned an impish smile at her, slid so they bumped elbows, then faced Mick. "What's her name?"

"Shelby, and don't scare her off. I gotta take care of some paperwork so I'll send Angel out."

"How can little ol' me scare anyone?" The girl's bright blue eyes—beautiful in an odd creepy way—widened innocently.

Mick snorted in reply as he walked off.

"Bad ass name. I love those cars." Lila nodded. "So where you from?"

"Texas." She hated when people made reference to her name. The car was cool. Being conceived in the backseat of one when your mom was sixteen wasn't.

Lila laughed. "Of course you are. That accent is almost as bad as a Tennessee or Georgia one."

Another small girl, with short, cropped, black hair came out of the back. She laid a shirt in front of her. Her porcelain skin made her storm-blue eyes stand out in her tiny face. "Mick said we have another waitress."

Lila didn't seem to notice the girl's cool demeanor. "This is Shelby, Angel. She's gonna help out tomorrow night."

"Of course. Be here at six." Angel frowned, narrowed her eyes and looked her up and down. With that the girl turned to bartend for the next customer.

"Is she my boss?" Shelby asked quietly. If so, she didn't think she'd work here long.

"No. Don't worry about her. She's just pissy about Thrand."

Angel's eyes swung towards them and narrowed.

"Don't look at me like that, Angel. You know damn well he was never into you."

Angel didn't respond, but her pale face turned pink.

"She's Mick's daughter. Anyway, I can't wait to work with you. Should be awesome. I better get back to it. See you tomorrow." With a waggle of her fingers she was off helping customers.

Shelby watched for a little while so she could get a feel for what was expected. It didn't look too hard. Take orders, place them at the bar, then deliver the drinks. Pretty simple.

It also gave her a minute to glance around the place. A small raised stage sat at the back. Tables and chairs were scattered here and there and the bar ran down the left side. Music played from the overhead speakers, but a band was setting up on the stage.

Hopefully, she would be able to keep up tomorrow night. She did *not* want to job hunt again.

The next night, she strode down Broadway. Memories of her and Gran walking along this very street lingered in her mind. She could hear Gran's voice telling her story after story of all the places that lined the famous strip. Gran grew up in Nashville so she knew everything there was to know. Or so it seemed to her as a child. Time had changed some things, but a lot had remained the same. Tootsies was still there with its neon sign and the Ryman was still around the corner. And Saturday nights were still non-stop and jammed with people on the sidewalks.

Booseys was just one in a long line of honky-tonks ready to serve up a drink and a country swagger. But she looked forward to doing something other than trying to make sense of Gran's dusty old belongings. Even if she did have to work.

Bouncers were in front of every bar, but she hesitated at the sight of the guy sitting at the door to Booseys. He was a heavyset man decked out in black leather with unruly hair and a beard. Thick heavy rings finished off his scary appearance. He made Mick look tame. He locked eyes with her.

"Shelby!" His booming voice made her jump. "I heard there was a new girl. No worries, doll." He chuckled and patted her hand. "I'm only scary to those who deserve it. I'm Dooley, by the way."

She wanted to ask how he knew her and then realized it was the Booseys shirt she was wearing. She managed a tentative smile and nodded. "Nice to meet you."

"Let me guess. Texas, right?"

"I never knew I had such an obvious accent." She pushed her hair behind her ear. She wished she didn't have a Texas accent. She would rather have lived her life with Gran. Perfectly content with a Tennessee one.

"You're a sweet one. But don't worry, hun. I don't bite." The twinkle in his eyes had her blushing. He squeezed her hand in reassurance, like he knew she needed it. "You have any trouble at all, just hunt me or Mick up. Got a feeling it's gonna be busier than usual."

"Thanks, Dooley." She turned and walked into the bar.

She glanced at the stage and stopped. The band setting up appeared to be anything but country. The singer was huge, sported black, mussed, spiky hair and tattoos that covered both arms from shoulder to wrist. He wore nothing but black, the gauges in his ears and a lip ring.

The rest of the band didn't seem very country either. The drummer wore a black cap on backwards, with gauges. The other two looked normal. Sort of. One wore rumpled clothes and had messy sandy blond hair—like he just rolled out of bed. The other had shaggy hair that hid his face. She glanced at the crowd full of cowboy hats and saw more than one scowl directed toward band.

She understood their confusion.

She spotted Lila waving at her, strode to the bar and picked up an apron.

Lila introduced Cassie, the girl standing next to her. She was stunning with long honeyed locks and a tall, curvy body. The girls were huddled together and the stark difference in their looks had heads turning their way.

The band, Cassie informed her, was called DirtSlap—Ethan, the lead singer, Zak, the bassist, Ryan, the guitarist and Thrand, the drummer. Country with a little dirt, she was told.

"You know a lot about the band," Shelby said to Cassie.

Lila sniggered. "She would. She's banging the drummer."

Cassie rolled her eyes and a blush hit her cheeks.

"You work here?" Shelby asked.

"Yeah, but I'm taking pictures tonight." She patted her camera bag. "Lila is the best. If you have any questions let her know."

"Thanks. I will."

Cassie walked to the stage, knelt in front of Ethan and snapped a picture.

Shelby tied off her apron and paused, fascinated by Ethan. He wasn't cute really—just different. Used to private schools, people who reeked of money and dressed the part, she was unaccustomed to people who looked like him—they didn't exist in her world. He wouldn't even be accepted in her circle. But very few people she'd met this week would.

She'd seen her fair share of boots and hats, she was from Texas after all, but it was all country club scene. Not the rough and tumble type who worked hard enough to get dirt on their jeans. She worried her lower lip. Her perspective was shifting. Was her life in Houston even real?

Shelby got to work filling orders. It was comparable to the college crowd on a Saturday night, until DirtSlap started playing. Until Ethan started singing.

Struck dumb, she stopped what she was doing and stared at him. Goosebumps spread over her skin. His voice was smooth, yet edgy. A Georgian accent with a hard rock vibe. Country with a little dirt. A very apt way of describing them.

He held a mic, stood feet planted wide and dominated the small stage. The crowd went silent. The band started their gig with popular country songs. They sounded nothing like the originals...DirtSlap made them their own.

She forced herself to get back to the task at hand, which was delivering drinks. It wasn't like she was a music junkie.

She'd only been to a handful of concerts in her entire life. All of which were country, in the strictest sense of the word, but seeing a guy who looked like Ethan croon a George Strait song was hypnotic.

It took all of about five songs before the place was so packed, she could barely move. She wasn't claustrophobic but even she was overwhelmed.

"Welcome to Booseys, ya'll," Ethan said into the mic. He pointed to each band member. "This is Ryan on guitar, Zak on bass, and the man behind the madness, Thrand on drums. I'm Ethan and we are DirtSlap." He grinned when some very girly screams echoed throughout the bar. "Be patient with the staff, ya'll. We weren't expecting this kind of crowd. But thanks for coming. Hope you like this next one. It's an original."

Shelby didn't realize she stared until an arm curled around hers. She looked down to see Lila's smiling face. "Told you. Amazing aren't they?"

Shelby nodded and wondered which one of the guys Lila was in love, or lust, with...whichever the case may be. By the look on her face, the girl crushed on at least one of them.

Although heavier than the covers, their original song still sounded country. The lyrics told a story about dirt roads and pick-up trucks, but it really showcased Ethan's voice as he let a little screamo escape now and then.

Lila sighed. "Guess we better get this crowd handled."

With only four waitresses working the floor, they were undermanned and outnumbered, but Shelby did her best she to keep up with demand. She served a group of guys in the corner of the bar and ignored their taunts and rude comments.

By the second time she passed them, one of the guys snagged her arm.

"Why don't you sit here and keep me company, sweet thing."

She looked up into his glassy eyes and shook her head. "Working, sorry."

The group of four laughed when she tried to pull away from the guy's grasp.

"You need to let me go," she demanded. Yelling wouldn't do any good in this madness.

He tugged so she had no choice but to fall against him. "See? I knew you wanted it."

She attempted to jerk free, but the drunken guy clamped his arm firmly around her waist. Frantic, she looked for Mick, but he was on the other side of the crowded room and couldn't see her.

"Let me go!" She elbowed the guy in the ribs hard enough she almost got loose, but not quite. The other guys laughed again and egged him on. Her throat constricted when his hand squeezed her ass.

A strong arm fell over her shoulder and pulled her to her feet. Pressed firmly against a very large, firm body, she breathed a sigh of relief.

Mick.

She craned her neck up.

It wasn't Mick.

Ethan was bigger up close. His dark shades hung in the neck of his sleeveless tee revealing his eyes. Bottomless black pools, accentuated by black eyeliner stared into hers. He gave her a wink a moment before his mouth landed on hers.

His lip ring was a hard contrast to her warm lips. Stunned, all she could do was gasp. His tongue swept against hers, and she shivered at the shocking metal bar of his tongue piercing. The tray she'd been holding like a weapon fell heedlessly to the floor.

He was sweaty, hot and for some unholy reason, she answered his kiss. Every shred of decency that had been force-fed into her was gone. A tiny part knew she should shove him away, but that part was lost in the uniqueness of being kissed by a man who obviously knew exactly what he was doing. His arm tightened and his hand angled her head so he could delve deeper.

The noise and the crowd faded into nothing. Nothing but a burn that spread all the way to her toes. And there was nothing she could do but cling to him so she wouldn't melt into a puddle at his feet.

He lifted his head, breaking the kiss, and reality smacked her in the face. The crowd roared in approval and she sucked in a breath. He turned his attention to the guys who had been harassing her and smiled at them—or more accurately, bared his teeth.

Ashlynn Pearce

Were it not for Hope, the Heart would Break...
Once upon a time...*You ain't gonna believe this shit!*
(I always wanted to start a bio like that!) But seriously—scrap
that, I'm not serious, but I do love to write. Create characters.
Give them hope that there is something better around the
corner. It's my passion. I live and breathe stories. When I'm
not arguing with the characters in my head (yes, I do that, you
can ask my hubby who thinks I'm nuts btw), I'm taking care of
said hubby, my two kids and a melee of furbabies. I'm Okie

born and bred and, yes, we get a lot of twisters and, no, there aren't any teepees around that I've seen.

Come on over, say hi and see what I'm up to!

www.AshlynnPearce.com[1]

FB: www.facebook.com/ashlynnpearcewriter[2]

Twitter: @Ashlynn_Pearce[3]

---

1. http://www.ashlynnpearce.com/

2. https://www.facebook.com/ashlynnpearcewriter

3. https://twitter.com/Ashlynn_Pearce

Don't miss out!

Visit the website below and you can sign up to receive emails whenever Ashlynn Pearce publishes a new book. There's no charge and no obligation.

https://books2read.com/r/B-A-GZDB-RHCE

Connecting independent readers to independent writers.

About the Author

Ashlynn Pearce

Were it not for Hope...the Heart would break...

Ashlynn Pearce writes fun and sexy romances. Born and bred in Oklahoma, she lives with her husband, son and four pups. She has overcome a lot in her life. With four strokes under her belt, she rides a Harley trike, is Gamaw her granddaughters and is working diligently on continuing her publishing dream.

After several visits to Nashville, she created the DirtSlap series. DirtSlap is a band - *a lil bit country, a dash of metal & a whole lot of dirt.* Included in the series are FUEL, WRECK, KRUSH and FIXT...with more coming.

If your looking hotter, leather and tattoos, look no further....Rolling Asylum Motorcyle Club series starting with On Edge coming Oct 28.

She loves to hear from her fans, so you can contact her at:

https://www.facebook.com/AshlynnPearceAuthor.

https://www.instagram.com/ashlynnpearceauthor/

tiktok: @ashlynnpearceauthor

Read more at https://ashlynnpearceauthor.com.